OUTLAW MARSHAL

Outlaw Marshal

Ray Hogan

THORNDIKE
CHIVERS

This Large Print edition is published by Thorndike Press, Waterville, Maine, USA and by BBC Audiobooks Ltd, Bath, England.
Thorndike Press, a part of Gale, Cengage Learning.

LIBRARY OF CONGRESS CATALOGING-IN-PUBLICATION DATA

Hogan, Ray, 1908–1998.
  Outlaw marshal / by Ray Hogan. — Large print ed.
    p. cm. — (Thorndike Press large print western.)
  ISBN-13: 978-1-4104-2354-2 (alk. paper)
  ISBN-10: 1-4104-2354-9 (alk. paper)
  1. Outlaws—Fiction. 2. Large type books. I. Title.
PS3558.O3473O98 2010
813'.54—dc22   2009048975

BRITISH LIBRARY CATALOGUING-IN-PUBLICATION DATA AVAILABLE

Published in 2010 in the U.S. by arrangement with Golden West Literary Agency.
Published in 2010 in the U.K. by arrangement with Golden West Literary Agency.

U.K. Hardcover: 978 1 408 49084 6 (Chivers Large Print)
U.K. Softcover: 978 1 408 49085 3 (Camden Large Print)

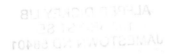

Printed in the United States of America
1 2 3 4 5 6 7 14 13 12 11 10

To LOIS
for patience and understanding

1

Santell was through, finished. He was going back to cattle country.

Crouched beside the narrow stream of snow water, he stirred impatiently. He could return now. Eva was out of his thoughts, gone from his mind. The wounds were healed over, and there remained only their leavening caution. But it had taken over a year to work her out of his system and wipe the memory of her from his mind, and the towering, silent Colorado mountains had been just the place to accomplish it. Eva, who once had meant all things to him, who had led him on and made him believe there was no other and then, one day, had brushed him lightly aside and married Tom Fallon, his best friend.

That same night he had climbed into his saddle and moved on, drifting with each change of the wind, coming finally to the hill country where he substituted a quest of gold for his fine dreams of Eva — and vowed to himself daily in the vast, limitless silence that no woman would ever again lead him on and play him for a sucker.

He straightened up, a tall, rangy man in typical Western dress with wide, powerful shoulders and a strong, square-cut face. The muscles of his legs, turned sharp by countless hunkerings along innumerable creeks in his fruitless search for yellow metal, twinged in protest. It stirred a deep growl of anger within him and temper flared through his frame. In a hasty, frustrated motion he flung his prospecting pan into the brush, setting up a clatter that sent half-a-dozen blue-coated camp robbers flapping for the nearest tree. He swung his glance toward a plume of smoke rising from beyond the hogback to the east. A town lay there — Sutterville, a passing pilgrim had informed him. A place where miners could buy supplies.

He wheeled away from the stream, his mind definitely made up. He would go there, dispose of his meager equipment and strike out for Texas, for the *Llanos Estacados* — the Staked Plains country. That's where he belonged, in a broad, rimless land where he could feel the hot sun on his back, the clean wind in his face. Where the nights were warm and soft and not bitter and laden with ice that cut a man to the bone. He was not cut out to be a miner, grubbing in the dirt or slopping around in the water. He needed the feel of a good horse working between his knees and the music of cattle bawling in his ears.

Swiftly he collected his belongings, tied them in his bed roll. He caught up the hobbled buckskin, fat as a Christmas pig on Colorado's sweet grass, and saddled him. In a few minutes he was aboard, pointing straight for the wisps of smoke trickling skyward.

First to Sutterville. Then eastward, eastward across the New Mexico flats to Texas.

2

South and some miles west of where Clay Santell had come to his decision, on the far side of a high-running ridge along a rough, faint track known as the Bitter Root trail, two men came to a halt. One, a tall, lean, powerfully built individual, looked much like Santell even to the clothing he wore except for the disfiguring scar that traced down his somewhat handsome face. He was Shotgun Travers, a killer, lately escaped from prison and now being returned.

The other, a small man, wore a gold-plated U. S. marshal's star. Only Harry

Decket was not really a U. S. marshal. He just affected such, playing the part when he was absent from his home country of Arizona where he was no more than a lowly, small-town peace officer.

The counterfeit role and the authority it mustered pleased him. It fed his monstrous, little-man's ego and he derived a vast amount of keen enjoyment from seeing other men bow to his will and leap to his beck and call. It was a minor thing anyway, he reasoned. His appointment to the coveted position could not be far off after the spectacular job he had exhibited in capturing Travers. He would not be an unnoticed nobody any longer. Everyone would be talking about him.

He swung his sharp, gray face to the outlaw, slouching in the saddle in that irritating, to-hell-with-it way of his. Travers was a big man, broad of shoulders, thick in body, and Decket had taken his full measure of delight in making him miserable all the way from Tucson. But he had an underlying and disturbing suspicion that Travers was far from impressed by it all and regarded him with curling contempt.

"When we eatin'?" Travers asked without turning.

"When I say so," Decket snapped acidly.

"Maybe when we get to Sutterville. Least-wise, I may be eating there. About you I'm not sure."

Travers came slowly about, regarding Decket with an aggravating half-grin. The long scar tracing down his left cheek from temple to chin showed whitely in the strong sunlight. "Just as you say, Mr. United States Marshal."

Decket felt a hot flush lift in his neck. Try as he would he could not keep Travers from riling him. Angrily, he said, "That's right! And see that you keep right on saying it that way. I got no orders to get you to Colorado alive — only to get you there. You keep your lip buttoned or there's liable to be an accident along the road!"

"Sure, sure," Travers murmured. "Call yourself President Rutherford Hayes for all I mind."

"Just you keep thinking that way and maybe you'll get where you're going alive."

Travers lifted his shaggy head and threw a speculative glance toward the towering Colorado peaks, blue-green in the hazy distance. "When you figure we'll get there?"

Decket's rapacious features were still. His eyes were small, black as anthracite; his nose sharp and beaklike. His mouth was scarcely a gray slash set always at a grim, hard line

11

and there was no humor anywhere in his makeup. He said, "Another week, maybe longer. Why? You in a big hurry, killer?"

"Nope," Shotgun Travers replied slowly. "No hurry at all. I was just wonderin' about it."

Decket's voice was heavy with suspicion. "You know this country?"

Travers shook his head. His hands were bound together with rawhide thongs, and now he raised them to brush back his hat, exposing a mass of brown hair. He mopped the collected sweat from his brow with his wrists. "Been through here once or twice, that's all," he said and let it drop.

It was a new world to Harry Decket, far removed from the flat, sandy cactus deserts of Arizona. Ever since they had left Santa Fe they had been in tall mountains, sometimes trailing across smooth and grassy valleys, other times moving along slowly over rough and rocky paths. At this point, far north and somewhat east of the settlement of Taos, they were deep in a wilderness of huge pines, upreaching spruce, ghostly aspens that whispered endlessly, and gigantic boulders and heat. Decket was learning that even at such altitude, the sun could be merciless.

"Thought this was where you did all your

hell raising."

Travers shook his head again. "Was farther north."

"Reckon these Colorado lawmen are going to be right glad to see you. You meandered a far piece, coming clear down into Arizona territory."

"My mistake," Travers said. "You were mighty lucky, Marshal, taking me the way you did."

Decket bristled at once, his thin shoulders coming up. "You call that luck?" he demanded hotly. "No luck to it! Just played it smart. When I heard you'd been seen coming my way, I set my trap. You walked into it, pretty as you please."

"Some trap," Travers grunted. "Sending a little kid out on the desert and then breaking his horse's leg. Anybody would stop to help a kid in trouble like that."

"Never hurt him any. And horses come cheap. What's important is, you fell for it."

"Like I said, anybody'd help a kid caught out there on the desert with a crippled horse, like he was."

"Maybe, but you being dumb helped a lot. You're like all big men, Travers. Big and stupid. Goes together. Bigger a man is the dumber he is."

The outlaw regarded him with flat, colorless eyes. "And bein' runty like you makes a man smart, I take it?"

Anger flashed through Decket. His diminutive size was ever a sore spot with him. He was a short man in a world of tallness. To be called runt or shorty or some similar term was, to him, a prime insult. In a lifting, trembling tone, he said, "Don't you ever call me that again, Travers! Not unless you want a bullet through your head!"

Travers gave him a slow, slanting grin. "Sure, Mr. United States Marshal. I won't ever call you a runt again."

Blind fury rushed through Harry Decket. A curse ripped from his lips and he jabbed spurs into his horse. The startled animal leaped forward and Decket, swinging his whip, slashed Travers across the neck and shoulders.

Like a huge, wounded bear, Travers growled deep. He came off the saddle, surprisingly fast for so big a man, and grabbed for the quirt. He missed by mere inches. Decket, his anger suddenly under control, wheeled hurriedly away on the narrow trail. He dragged out his pistol and leveled it threateningly at the outlaw.

"All right, settle down," he managed in a voice that still shook slightly. He had almost made a mistake, a bad one, and one thing

Harry Decket hated to do was make a mistake of any sort. If Travers had succeeded in getting his hands on that whip and jerking. . . .

Travers stared at the pistol, its fancy scrolled-silver surfaces flashing in the bright noonday sun. After a moment he shrugged his powerful shoulders in a show of defeat. "Better not try that again, Marshal," he said in a low, normal voice. "Maybe I'll get my hands on you and if ever I do, I'll sure tear that cocky head of yours off your puny body and stomp it into the ground."

"Maybe," Decket replied, trying to appear unmoved by the cool warning, "but don't you do any dreaming about it. There's five bullets in this gun and they can all travel faster than a big ox like you. One false turn by you and I'll prove it."

"Doubt that," Travers drawled insolently. "I know you don't have to get me to Colorado still living, but I know you sure want to. Means more glory for you, taking me in on foot. Makes your chances for getting a real, genuine U.S. marshal's badge a lot better."

Decket's bloodless lips curled downward. "Well, well, maybe you're smarter than I've been giving you credit for! Didn't figure you had sense enough to see that. But don't let it give you ideas. Maybe I would prefer to deliver you to the law alive but I just don't really have to. I got to deliver one Shotgun Travers, dead or alive, it don't matter much, not to me or to Colorado."

Travers was not listening. He had simply turned away and now he stood with his back to the marshal, his gaze on the far off peaks. After a time he laid his pinioned hands upon the saddle horn and prepared to swing up. "Sure getting powerful hungry," he muttered. "Let's move on."

"Hold it!" Decket commanded, his eyes going small and sharp as another of his ideas came to him. "Expect you might be needing a bit of exercise before you eat. Let's just do a spell of walking. Few miles will do you good."

Travers swung a startled glance to him. He looked down at his high-heeled boots and then ahead to the rocky, uneven trail winding off the ridge. "Hell, Marshal, I can't walk in these boots —" he said in a disgusted voice.

"Try it barefooted," Decket suggested sarcastically. "Come on, get moving!"

Travers covered him with a withering sweep of his empty eyes and pushed up to the front of his horse. Taking up the reins, he started along the difficult pathway,

16

stumbling awkwardly over its uneven surface. "Man's got a mean streak a yard wide," he mumbled, already beginning to breathe heavily from his efforts.

Decket, barely overhearing, snapped, "What's that?"

But Shotgun Travers was no complete fool. "Nothin'," he muttered, shaking his head. He had had enough of Decket's twisted sense of justice for the time.

Harry Decket gloated inwardly. He was enjoying the spectacle of the big man staggering and reeling along, glorying in the knowledge that he, and he alone, had such absolute power over the outlaw. It was a good feeling. It was like a man handling a stubborn mule, he mused, bending the powerful brute to his own will, forcing it to do as he wished. After all, size was not everything. Brains and a six gun at a man's side equalized all things, assuming the man had the guts to use both. He watched Travers with slow contempt. He should really be grateful to the outlaw; Travers was his ladder to bigger, higher things, his key to unlocking the door of the future. After this would come the job as county sheriff and after that, U. S. marshal. Maybe it would even be possible to skip the sheriff part and bounce right to the top of the

profession in one leap. It had been done
before and by men with much less aptitude
than he. And now, with his reputation as a
tough lawman enhanced many degrees by
the delivering of Shotgun Travers to the
authorities in Colorado, anything could be
possible.

Decket compressed his lips. They were dry
and he moistened them with his tongue,
savoring at the same time the prospects of
such glorious success. A fine thread of thrill-
ing delight traced through him as he envi-
sioned what others would say, how they
would look at him in a sort of awe. Unconsciously he drew his thin shape higher, a bit
more erect in the saddle.

Yes, he really should thank Travers for
making such probabilities a possibility. He
decided then and there that he would; he
would thank him by keeping him alive,
although perhaps suffering every step of the
way. That would prove one more thing to
everybody. That he was a firm and just law
officer, taking no nonsense from any man,
be he large or small, timid or desperate. And
more proof that he deserved to wear the
star of a United States marshal.

He glanced ahead to Travers, stumbling
along in front of his horse. He frowned
slightly. This was consuming a lot of good

time and, after all, he had made his point. He was certain there was no doubt now in the outlaw's mind as to who was bossing this trip. They should be moving faster; the sooner he got Travers to the Colorado authorities, the quicker he could get back to Arizona and the closer he would be to his commission. He opened his mouth to yell at Travers. In that same fragment of time, the outlaw wheeled and leaped off the trail. He disappeared into a gully eight feet below, horse and all.

Decket clawed frantically at the gun at his hip and snapped a hurried shot at the escaping Travers. But the outlaw had chosen a good place to make his break. It was a blind turn in the trail offering immediate cover. Decket's horse, frightened by the exploding gun, reared and backed away from the unexpected noise, pawing at the air with his forelegs.

In a single, flashing moment Harry Decket saw his ambitions vanishing into vapor. He cringed inwardly, seeing the disgrace and humiliation and ridicule that would descend upon him when it became known he had lost his prisoner. It seared through him like a furious, white-hot knife. It couldn't happen to him! It must not — not when he was so close to attaining the goal he wanted so badly!

Savagely he jammed spurs to his horse and sawed at the bit. The horse came down on all fours and Decket drove him to the edge of the bluff, roweling him brutally as he tried forcing him to leap. The animal was wild with fear, half-crazed from the gouging bit and jabbing spurs. He continued to shy away, pull back.

"Jump! Jump, damn you!" Decket screamed, beating the horse senselessly about the ears with his quirt.

The horse finally went off the ledge, striking heavily on his front legs and going momentarily to his knees. Decket hauled him up by the reins, throwing quick glances down the arroyo through which Travers must have traveled. It was a deep, narrow gash doubling back along the trail but at a much lower level. The prints of the outlaw's horse were plain, sunk deeply into the soft sand.

Slashing his mount unmercifully with the whip, Decket began his pursuit. Travers could not have gone far, he reasoned, not with his hands tied together and being out of the saddle at the time of the break. But he'd lost time fighting with that fool horse, trying to get him off the trail. That had worked in the outlaw's favor. He tried to listen, tried to hear the sounds of Travers' flight. There was nothing but the noises of his own crashing progress through the brush, the creak of his saddle and the labored breathing of his own horse.

He broke into an open area, a junction of two other arroyos. He should be able to see Travers from that point, he could not be far ahead now. And when Decket caught up with him, he'd make Travers wish he'd never thought of escape! He would add that to his reputation, too. He would make it known far and wide that Harry Decket was a man you had better not try to run from.

But he saw nothing, only brush, sand and emptiness. Worse yet, the tracks ended right there. They left the loose sand, climbed up onto a rocky incline and were gone, heading apparently into the dark and shadowy depths of piñon and oak brush that matted the hillside lifting to his right.

Decket again tried listening, straining to catch every sound. The forest was a silent tomb. And then, far to the righthand, a bluejay began to chatter and scold. It seemed to Decket the bird was deliberately mocking him, and he began to curse in a muttering stream.

He drove bloody spurs into his heaving

horse again and rode hard for the top of a low mound a few hundred yards distant. From that vantage point he could better see the network of arroyos and gullies fanning out like a many-fingered hand. He checked them carefully one by one. The only sign of life was a thin-coated, half-starved coyote skulking in the shade of a doveweed bush, watching him with dull, yellow eyes. He turned his attention back to the slope. There was no seeing into its labyrinth of dark shadows.

Travers could have taken any one of a dozen directions; Harry Decket admitted that to himself as he studied the silent hillside. The man could be anywhere! Damn a country where you couldn't see more than a hundred feet away! Down in the desert country, a man could see for miles! A frustrated curse ripped from the marshal's lips. And he had been so close — so near to gaining the one thing he wanted most!

But it was not over yet. The last verse had not yet been sung. Travers was not scot free, not by a broad sight. He could be found, and if Harry Decket had one good quality, it was that of tenacity when he was on the trail of a wanted man. They might duck and dodge and hide but they could not do it forever. And Shotgun Travers was no exception. It might take all the rest of the summer, into next year, even. But he could be found. He would be found!

Decket sawed his horse about and drove for the trail, a plan shaping up in his mind. He would go on to Sutterville and draft a posse; get a tracker if there was one to be had. They could be back on the trail before dark and Travers could not possibly get very far by that time. He lashed at the laboring horse beneath him, his jaw a hard, bitter line. No sonofabitch was going to make him a laughingstock!

3

Santell pulled the buckskin to a halt at the end of Sutterville's single street and let his weary gaze run the row of weathered, neglected buildings. It was a small town, not over two dozen structures at the most in its scoured makeup, but it looked like paradise to him after a night and the better part of a day's riding across the mountains. Any place where he could buy a meal and rent a bed was fine with him.

This was the last town he would see in the mountain country. It lay at the very edge of the mountains, two-thirds of the way up a lengthy, sprawling slope. From where he sat Santell could look out beyond the town, past the rim of trees, and see the flat prairies unrolling southward and to the east, toward Texas where he belonged.

Once again his eyes searched the street. He was a big, wide-shouldered man with a wedge-shaped torso, wearing faded levis and a checkered wool shirt that was open down the front exposing a dark shield of fine, glossy hair. He brushed his wide-brimmed hat, a relic of his range-riding days, to the back of his head and frowned. First he would buy the supplies he needed for the trail. Then he would have that big platter of steak and potatoes rounded off by a big slice of apple pie. He had been thinking about that all the way across the mountain. After that he'd have a couple of drinks and turn in. With a good night's rest behind him, the kind that comes from sleeping on a mattress and springs, he would feel like an early start next morning. And he could ride far.

A squat rock-and-wood building with the sign, GENERAL MERCHANDISE, A. Gamble, Prop., drew his attention. He turned his pony toward it, drawing up at the hitching rail. He swung down, his flat-heeled Hyer boots, badly worn and scuffed, shooting out puffs of dust when his feet hit the dry ground. A gun belt encircled his slim waist, the pistol hanging low on his right leg. It was thonged to him just above the knee, not for quick drawing but rather for the more practical purpose of preventing its slapping when he walked.

He climbed the four steps to the porch and entered the store, moving with the easy, confident swing of a healthy man toughened by the extremes of nature. The storekeeper peered at him suspiciously over the tops of his spectacles and wiped his fingers on the bib of an apron.

"How do."

Santell nodded to the salutation, alert to the close caution in the storekeeper's attitude. It was understandable; he hadn't shaved in three days and he knew he presented a hard-lined, forbidding appearance. Santell glanced casually along the shelves of merchandise.

"Don't recollect seein' you around here afore," the storekeeper observed.

"First time through," Santell said shortly.

He felt the man's probing eyes taking their curious inventory of him. Irritated finally, he snapped, "You here to do business or just gawk?"

Gamble swallowed hard. "Do business, I reckon. What can I do for you, Mister?"

Santell bought coffee, a half-side of bacon,

some tinned goods and a few other staples, all suitable for the trail. When he was finished he said, "How about throwing that in a flour sack for me?"

Gamble ducked his head. His gaze came to rest on the gun at Santell's hip. "That belt of your'n is about empty. How about a box of ca'tridges?"

"Forty-fours," Santell said.

He turned then and sauntered to the doorway and looked out. Locating the bank he noted its drawn blinds and closed entrance. He had intended transacting a small amount of business there but the place appeared closed. Without turning he said, "When's the bank open?"

The storekeeper said, "Should be open right now. Reckon George Miller's out somewheres."

Santell had five ten-dollar gold pieces left. In the interest of having smaller coins for paying his needs in the small villages through which he would be traveling, he had planned to convert them before he started. "Anybody else around there? Maybe living in the back or upstairs?"

Gamble, in the act of looping a noose about the neck of the flour sack, came to a full stop. He stared at Santell closely, his small eyes pulling down into tiny, thoughtful slits. Under the ruddiness of his stitched skin a paleness seeped through and began to show. "Why, I reckon I don't know," he stammered. "I just ain't sure about that."

Santell shrugged and came back to the counter. He laid a gold piece before the man and picked up the handful of silver change returned to him. He could skip the bank. He had some small coins now. Maybe they would last him until he reached the next town of any size. He slung the bag of groceries over his arm and moved back to the street, feeling the hard drill of Gamble's eyes on his shoulders as he crossed the porch.

He hesitated beside his horse. Remembering the shells for his gun, he opened the sack and took out the box, stuffing it into his pocket. He then secured the bag to the saddle and pulling loose the reins, led the tired buckskin to the stables. He walked into the runway and a short, thin man emerged from the gloomy depths of stalls and passageways to meet him.

Santell passed over the leathers. "Rub him down. Good. I want him to have plenty of grain. He's come a long way and he'll be going a lot farther."

The hostler said, "Yes, sir!" in a quick, businesslike manner.

"Put him here in this front stall so I'll know just where he is. Leave the tack in there with him. I may want to pull out when you're not around. How much?"

"Dollar'll do it."

Santell flipped the coin to the stableman. He spun about and started for the door. Over his shoulder he said, "In case you're the nosey kind, there's nothing in that flour sack but grub."

The hostler said, "Yes, sir," this time in a sheepish, falling voice and regarded Santell owlishly.

Santell came again into the full sunlight, feeling better by the minute as the exercise out of the saddle began to relax his jaded muscles. He stood for a time near the corner of the livery barn, indulging in a longtime habit of absorbing his surroundings. His world was made up of what he saw and heard and could taste or smell, or feel with his broad, strong hands. All things to him meant something, were part of a pattern — an overheard word, a swiftly closing door, a riderless horse walking slowly down a deserted street, the break in a woman's eyes when she turned away. In some final conclusion each had its meaning, a substance, a bearing upon an outcome, a point for or against life or death. And each received his deep and thoughtful consideration for he was a man intensely interested in his world and all the people and things in it.

His attention came to halt on a knot of men and horses gathered in front of the sheriff's office a hundred yards or so down the way. He studied them for some minutes, deciding some new and unusual event had pulled them together, and then he swung toward the hotel. Whatever it was, he was bound to hear about it sooner or later. That was the way of it in small towns. Things passed swifter than lightfall. Right then, however, he was interested in hiring a room, washing up and getting a bite to eat. After that he would either go on to bed or perhaps, if he felt just right, he might take in a little of Sutterville's night life.

He entered the single-storied, rambling affair and crossed the empty lobby. The clerk, lounging behind a desk that badly needed paint, greeted him with a hesitant nod of his head. He was a young man, round-faced and flat-nosed, and he wore a striped shirt with a high, celluloid collar but no necktie. He wore black satin sleeve guards that reached above his elbows.

"How about a room?"

The clerk nodded woodenly, his colorless eyes glued to Santell. He pushed a dog-eared book across the desk and reached a stub of pencil from behind his ear.

Santell considered the finger-tracked page for a moment, aware of the clerk's steady gaze. Anger brushed through him. He lifted his glance suddenly, gray eyes smouldering beneath their shelf of black brows. "What the hell's the matter with you? First customer this hotel has ever had?"

The clerk's stare dropped. He gulped noisily. Santell turned again to the register and wrote, C. Santell, Brazos, Texas, in a broad, heavy hand.

"What room?"

"Take Number Two," the clerk murmured. "Second door on your left."

Santell located his quarters and pushed into their stuffy depths. The place had been shut up for days, apparently. He stepped to the window, raising both the discolored, torn shade and wooden sash, letting in a gush of fresh air. Maybe by the time he got to bed, it would clear out. He poured himself a bowl of water from the china pitcher and scrubbed at his whisker-rough face. He should shave, he thought, but he had left his razor in the saddlebags and was of no mind to go after it now. He would remember to pick it up on his way back from eating and take time in the morning to scrape off his beard. Drying off, he went again into the street. He located the town cafe and crossed over to it. The sign hanging at a crazy angle over its door said, CHRISMAN'S, in large block letters and below that in smaller print, ALL KINDS OF FOOD ATE HERE.

Santell studied the sign for a moment and then entered, still speculating on its meaning. Two men were the only other customers. They were sitting at the short counter drinking coffee. Santell took a place on the bench at the opposite end. A man, evidently Chrisman, came from the back, wiping his hands on his apron and took Santell's order: steak, potatoes, beans, coffee and pie. The coffee now. Chrisman drew a thick mug of black liquid and placed it before him.

"Be a few minutes before the steak's done," he said.

Santell nodded. "All right."

"— he's the U. S. Marshal from Arizona," one of the men at the other end of the counter was saying. "Name of Harry Decket."

"Where'd this here Shotgun Travers give him the slip at?"

"Somewhere close to Bitter Root Ridge, near as I can figure." The man paused, wagging his head. "Sure hate to be that Travers.

31

I'll bet Decket's a tough little rooster when he gets riled. Sure wouldn't want him ridin' my tail."

"Who's heading up the posse?"

"Jake Perrick. He's the closest thing we got to a lawman since the sheriff's off in Denver. They're startin' out soon as they can find old Charley Ironhead. Need him to do the trackin'."

Santell's consciousness gathered in the conversation. An escaped prisoner somewhere in the hills nearby. A man named Travers had got away from the U. S. Marshal whose name, it appeared, was Harry Decket. Sutterville's sheriff was out of town and somebody by the name of Jake Perrick was making up a posse to help the marshal.

The cafe owner brought his platter of food, heaped to the edges. Santell looked it over with the obvious appreciation of a man near sick to death of his own cooking.

"Looks mighty tempting," he said aloud, picking up knife and fork. "First decent meal I've had in weeks."

He started to eat, realizing the two men had ceased their talking, that they were regarding him narrowly. He gave them a hard, brief glance. What the devil was wrong with this town, anyway? People in it acted like they never before had seen a stranger.

■ ■ ■ ■

"What's the holdup?" Marshal Harry Decket threw his impatient question at Jake Perrick. "Wasted more than two hours here now. Come on, let's get on with it!"

Perrick said, "Yes sir, Mr. Decket. I know you been waitin' but there just ain't no use startin' without the Indian. We got to have him to do the trailin'. He's the best in the country and there's no use tryin' to find this Travers without him."

Charley Ironhead, half Arapaho, half Mexican. An outcast from both peoples, he was usually to be found somewhere about Sutterville either sleeping off a drunk or else trying to cadge enough silver change to go on one. But he was the best trailer to be had, and Decket knew it would be foolish to leave without him. However, it pleased him to show his irritation at the delay; it kept the men scurrying around trying to please him, pinned them to their places of servitude.

He lounged against the doorway of the jail, his narrow, dour face toward Jake Perrick. Perrick, another huge, bulky man, had drawn his automatic dislike at the very start and this was greatly aggravated by the fellow's slovenly appearance. Decket was clean to the point of being finicky; he glared at Perrick's unshaven cheeks, at the stain of tobacco juice in the corners of his mouth. His shirt had not been changed in weeks and his fawn gray breeches were a greasy, slick brown, dappled with food stains. He wore a ridiculous, narrow brimmed hat of black felt and a corduroy coat that was ripped out at both armpits. The pockets bulged with various items he saw fit to carry along.

Decket had figured Jake Perrick out quickly: a man whose main thoughts were of himself, whose biggest weakness was women and who had catered to it until his eyes had grown cloudy, his mouth loose and flabby. Decket's glance swung from him in disgust. A fine thing to deputize as a lawman! But it was the best he could do. Perrick was some sort of a jackleg deputy for one of the big mines in the area, and with the sheriff gone there wasn't any better choice.

Actually, the two other men he had deputized and who now stood near their horses awaiting the word to mount up looked more like lawmen. One, Tex London, was a tall, drawling redhead. The other, called Sam Cunningham, was an older, graying man who kept to himself. Sam was the best man of the three, Decket had decided in his hasty, arbitrary way. He should be the leader of the posse and not that fat hog of a Perrick. At least Cunningham looked clean. Even London made a better appearance. But London's kind came a dime a dozen; men who could never think for themselves, who had to be told what to do and just when to do it. They were no good unless you rode their backs constantly.

He let his slitted eyes drift down the street beyond the pair. He came suddenly to a fine, sharp attention. A man, a big man, was mounting the steps to the hotel. There was something vaguely familiar about his build, about the way he carried himself as he walked. And then Decket's nerves relaxed. It was not Shotgun Travers. It had looked something like him from the distance — big, heavy, shoulders pitched forward, the slant of his wide-brimmed hat, the swing of his thick arms. But it wasn't Travers.

Perrick sidled up to him. "Indian'll be here in ten, fifteen minutes. What say we all go have a drink before we start?"

Decket gave that his deliberate consideration. "All right," he said as if granting a great favor, "I'll go along with you." He stepped out of the jail.

Behind him Perrick said, "Come on, boys," to London and Sam Cunningham and they all moved off toward the saloon. Decket walked slightly ahead of the others, not liking to be in the center of the group; the tallness of the other three men accented his own shortness.

Decket selected a table near the bar and they all sat down. One of the girls strolled up and Perrick rose and drew her aside a few steps for a short conversation. The bartender brought a bottle and four glasses and placed them in front of the marshal. Perrick came back to his seat, his yellow teeth bared in a wide grin.

"Little story I was tellin' Maisie," he explained. "About a couple of miner's who'd been holed up —"

"Forget it," Decket snapped. He was in no mood for jokes of any sort, particularly one of Perrick's sort. The loss of Travers rankled him deeply, and the delay in getting on the man's trail was adding vinegar to the wound. He poured himself a shot of the whisky and began to twirl it between his fingers, watching the amber fluid slosh gently about. He wished that big man going into the hotel had been Travers! He would mighty quick clap his hands on him and get out of this lousy town!

Tex London said, respectfully, "How long you been a U. S. marshal, Mr. Decket?"

Decket lifted his gaze to the deputy. Maybe Tex wasn't such a blockhead after all. He knew what it meant to be a U. S. marshal. He shrugged broadly, "Quite a spell, son."

"Takes a lot of experience to get that job," Jake Perrick observed.

There was a slight commotion across the room from them, near the batwing doors. Perrick screwed about in his chair to look. It was Amos Gamble, the storekeeper. He caught the man's searching glance just as he asked, "Anybody here seen Jake?"

"Over here, Amos," Perrick called.

Gamble pushed hurriedly through the scatter of tables. He nodded to Decket and the others and then drew up a chair, his face bright with excitement. "Jake, you actin' as sheriff, I figured I ought to tell you this. You too, Mr. Decket. I think I saw this here Travers you're looking for!"

Decket watched the man with veiled amusement. Shotgun Travers right here in Sutterville? Not if he knew Travers.

"Feller came into my place a little while ago. Big man, pretty well fits the description you passed out, Mr. Decket. Bought himself some groceries and a box of forty-four ca'tridges. Stranger to me and I figure I know everybody in this part of the country."

"Just bein' big and a stranger don't make him this Travers," Perrick said with a shake of his head.

"Somethin' else was right funny. Asked about the bank. Wanted to know why it was closed and if anybody lived in the back of it. Acted to me like he was thinkin' about bustin' into it!"

Perrick frowned. After a moment he again shook his head. "Travers wouldn't risk coming here. Too close to where he give the marshal the slip."

Harry Decket's sharp face was a mask concealing the idea that was rising in his cunning mind. He knew the man the store-keeper was talking about; he certainly was not Shotgun Travers although he did resemble him slightly. But if he was a total stranger to Sutterville. . . . The idea catapulted suddenly into a plan that would save him time, perhaps even the disgrace and humiliation of having lost a prisoner should Travers somehow manage to escape for good. But he would have to proceed carefully; he would have to let Perrick and the others build the case for themselves — and him.

He said, "Well, I don't know about that.

This Travers is plenty long on nerve. Got more than his fair share. Besides, where else could he go for supplies if he wanted to light out and travel? Any other towns around close?"

"Good two days off to the next one," Tex London said.

Perrick thought for a long minute. "Reckon we better not overlook it, Marshal," he agreed. He swung back to Gamble. "Anybody else see this here stranger, Amos?"

"Went from my place to Coaley's. Left his horse there then went to the hotel. Little while after that he crossed over to Chrisman's. I suspect he's still there, eatin'.."

Perrick ducked his head at Tex London. "Go tell Coaley to come over here. And stop at the hotel and tell Willie I want to see him, too."

The cowboy arose and left at once. Perrick rubbed doubtfully at his whiskery chin. "Still don't make good sense, him comin' here."

Decket sipped at his drink. "Most outlaws don't make good sense, anyway. Otherwise they wouldn't be outlaws. Could be Travers thinks I'm still back there along that ridge searching for him. He hasn't seen me around town yet."

The hotel clerk came into the saloon at that point, bustling with new-found importance. He dropped into Tex London's chair and leaned his elbows on the table. Before Perrick could speak, he said, "You know what, Jake, I had the same idea about that big jasper as Amos. This Santell, as he signed himself on the book, is sure the spittin' like of the marshal's escaped prisoner."

"That so?" Perrick murmured. "Appears Tex told you all about it."

"Told me what Amos said. But I already had my own ideas. Stranger. Big man, tough as all get out. And not travelin' with any baggage either. Just what he had on his back and a gun."

"Here's Coaley," Cunningham broke in.

Perrick turned to face the stableman. "I reckon Tex already told you what this is all about, too. You talk to this stranger?"

Coaley nodded. "Mighty little talkin' I did. He done the most of it. Give me strict orders about that horse of his. How I was to feed him and leave the gear in the stall with him and bed him down in the front where he would be handy. Said he might be leavin' in a hurry maybe when I wasn't around."

Decket's gaze slid from one man to another, studying their faces, seeing their convictions grow. It was like a snowball; it had begun with one small suspicion and then built rapidly as, one by one, more seemingly pertinent facts were jostled about to fit the pattern. They were providing him with a Shotgun Travers, ready made to take the place of the one that had escaped. Of course, he would have to forego the honor of delivering this one alive to the authorities in Colorado; they undoubtedly would know what the real Travers looked like. But that was a minor detail easily remedied. Tomorrow, somewhere along the trail, this prisoner would also try to escape and would get a bullet for his pains. It would all sound natural enough; hadn't Travers already tried to escape once before? He would then bring the body back to Sutterville, let them all see it, after which it would be buried. Jake Perrick, acting as a law officer for the town, would sign the death certificate attesting to the fact that it was Shotgun Travers. It would be easy.

Perrick said, "Well, could be somethin' to all this, Mr. Decket. What do you think?"

The marshal scratched at his ear. "I'll admit it sounds like Travers. Guess there's just one sure way to find out," he said then, voicing the obvious. "Let's go have a look at him. If it's him, I'll sure recognize him."

41

Jake Perrick wagged his head. "Saved us a lot of gab if we'd thought of that in the first place. Where'd you say he was now, Amos?"

"Eatin'. Over at Chrisman's."

Decket got to his feet, the others hastening to follow. They moved across the room and out into the street, pausing there in the sunlight.

"Chrisman's Cafe is over there, Marshal," Perrick said, pointing to the small building across the street and down fifty yards or so.

Two horses stood at the rail in front of it. Decket could not see beyond the small, curtained windows and he studied the structure for some time. "That place got a back door?"

Perrick said, "Yeh. Opens off into the alley."

"Put a man back there in case it is Travers and he tries to make a break again. We'll go in by the front." He stopped, letting his eyes sweep the remaining men. "Rest of you stay clear. I don't want nobody getting hurt here."

They crossed the separating distance in a thin group, Decket and Perrick somewhat in the lead. When they reached the restaurant, Tex London moved off to a position at the rear. While they waited for this to be done Harry Decket checked his gun, his small, close-set eyes jet black and fathom-less, his thin mouth a hard, colorless line. Nodding to Perrick he pulled back the door and stepped inside. One man sat at the counter, a half-empty coffee cup in his hand. It was the big fellow he had seen entering the hotel.

Chrisman appeared from the back of the building at the door's slam. He stopped short, seeing the marshal and Jake Perrick. At a shake of the latter's head, he eased back out of sight, slipping finally through the rear exit into the alleyway.

Harry Decket turned slightly to meet Perrick's inquiring glance, adjusting his position so that his face might also be seen by those who were waiting outside. He nodded. Immediately he came back around to the man at the counter, a wicked satisfaction glittering in his eyes. He let his hand drop to the gun at his side.

"All right, Travers!" he barked. "Don't move!"

4

Clay Santell looked up in surprise.

"Keep your hands on top that counter! One false move out of you, Travers, and you're a dead man!"

43

The impact of the words were like a solid hammer blow to Santell. For a long moment he sat as if frozen. Then a smile crossed his darkly tanned face. He met the hard, thrusting gaze of the man who wore a marshal's star and his companion.

"You got your ropes crossed up somewhere," he said slowly. "My name's not Travers. It's Santell."

The marshal moved a step closer. His hand rested on the butt of his pistol. The other man slid in behind him. Outside a murmuring group of people had gathered near the door.

"Get up!" the marshal ordered harshly. "I've wasted enough time around here now. Your escape didn't pan out like you figured. Now drop it and don't try playing cozy with me — or by heaven, I'll drop you where you stand!"

The perplexity and amazement in Santell began to give way to anger. This couldn't be happening to him, this being arrested as an escaped prisoner. He surely did not look so much like Shotgun Travers as to be taken for him by the very man who had been his captor. Yet — here it was actually taking place! He searched the grim face of the marshal, a dull suspicion growing suddenly within him.

"My name is Santell. Clay Santell. It's not Travers or anything else. I'm not your prisoner and I never was. I've been up in the hills doing a mite of prospecting and now I'm on my way back to Texas."

Decket surveyed him completely. He laughed, a harsh, mocking sound. "Sure — you're not Travers. You maybe look just exactly like him. I've been around you night and day for near to a month and I don't even know you when I see you. But just to please you — how about some proof that your name is Santell or whatever you call yourself."

The marshal had a thin smirk lying across his lips as if he already knew the answer to that question. Santell, studying the slyness in the man's small eyes, realized more lay here then showed on the surface, that there was something deeper and beyond his understanding. And he was powerless to fight it. He looked slowly about, thinking fast of escape, judging his chances. He said, "I'm a stranger in this town; I suspect you know that. Closest friend I've got who could stand for me is in Texas. Town called Splendor."

"Two or three days away," the big man with the marshal commented dryly. That man would probably be Jake Perrick, Santell thought, remembering the overheard conversation of the two cafe customers. Decket would be the name of the marshal.

"And what am I supposed to be doing while you run over after your friend — just set here and wait?" Decket demanded with a fine show of sarcasm.

Perrick laughed. There was an echoing snicker from the cluster of townspeople beyond the screen door. Decket folded his arms across his chest and rocked gently on his heels. A voice which Santell recognized as that of Gamble, the storekeeper, came in from the yard: "I knew 'twas him! Knew 'twas that Travers the minute he walked into my store!"

Santell cast around in his mind for some answer to the moment, something other than violence. The first blush of surprise and then anger had faded and now he was feeling the desperateness of his position. There was nothing he could produce to identify himself. He had no papers, no letters or cards that had been written him. He checked mentally through his saddlebags. There was nothing there either. He knew no one in the entire area; a lone prospector makes no friends. Hall McGivern, he had heard a few months back, had taken on the job as town marshal of the Texas settlement

Splendor, and it had been to him he had referred. But he was not even sure of that. It was only a passing rumor, for all he knew. And there was no one else north of Abilene with whom he was acquainted.

Stalling for time he said, "How about you checking with the marshal in Splendor? I'd be willing to stick around until you found out for sure."

Perrick laughed. "He'd be willing to stick around! How about that, Marshal!"

"Take a good four days to do that," Decket said with a shake of his head. "I want to be fair about this but —"

Perrick drew his gun. "What's all the arguing for? The marshal says you're his man and he sure ought to know. I think we done enough jawing."

Perrick waved his gun toward the doorway. Decket said, "You're right. Been enough time wasted here. Let's get moving."

Santell was watching the marshal closely. He was reading the narrow lines of Harry Decket's face, seeing the cruelty, the razor-sharp cunning that made up its angles and planes. A thought that had been tagging his mind pushed to the fore, shocking him with its implications: Decket knew he was not Shotgun Travers! It could be no other way. Maybe Perrick and the others were unaware

47

of it, just taking the marshal's word for it, but Harry Decket knew! Suddenly it became clear to him. Decket had carelessly allowed his prisoner to escape. Now he was trying to make a substitution to save his own face and reputation.

And he had chosen Santell as that substitute.

Immediately a further conclusion became startlingly clear: since the prison authorities or whoever Decket was delivering his prisoner to would know the real Shotgun Travers, the marshal's plan could not call for his being handed over alive.

A coolness began to flow through Santell. Now that he had his understanding of the problem, now that he knew the extent of the danger he faced, he could think and act clearly. He watched the slovenly bulk of Jake Perrick start toward him. His glanced flicked the two lawmen. He made his estimate of their values. Decket would be the dangerous one.

"This is your mistake," he said then in a slow, drawling voice that carried a cool warning.

Perrick halted. Decket said, "Mistake was yours, Travers. You made it back there on the trail. No man ever got away from me. You're not going to be the first!"

"Maybe," Santell said softly and threw the coffee, cup and all, straight at the two men. He whirled about and lunged through the back door, colliding with a man standing there. The crash bowled the lighter man over like a ten pin. Perrick's strangled yell sounded behind him. He drew his gun and snapped a shot through the still-open back door. There was a clattering noise as the bullet smashed into a stack of dishes.

He raced on down the alleyway, swung right into a narrow passage that led to the street. To the rear of him more shouts were coming from the yard around the cafe. Boots were pounding along the hardpack. He reached the street and paused. A buck-skin horse stood at a rail a dozen steps away. There was no hope of reaching his own mount in time. Without hesitation he lunged across the open space, yanked the reins free of the bar and vaulted into the saddle. Wheeling the pony about, he sped off down the dusty street.

"Get him!" Harry Decket's voice shrilled frantically from somewhere behind.

A gun crashed through the still, hot air. Santell heard the whine of a bullet nearby. He crouched lower in the saddle and drew his own pistol. Twisting about, he laid a quick shot at the cluster of men just emerging from the passageway through which he had raced. The bullet dug dust before them and they scattered like startled quail. He turned back to the buckskin, keeping him pointed down the road.

More guns began to crack. He caught the moan of lead close by again. He reached the open road and the little horse lengthened his stride, giving his best. There was one bullet left in his pistol. He threw a glance over his shoulder. Decket and the others had reached the jail where their horses waited. Somebody procured a rifle and the marshal was at that moment sighting carefully down its long, shining barrel. Santell leveled his last shot at the man, hoping to spoil his aim. But Decket was a cool one. He did not flinch when Santell's lead spouted dirt near him. Santell saw then a tiny puff of smoke from the rifle and in the same instant felt a searing along his side, just below his left armpit. He had been hit; he realized it at once. But it was scarcely more than a burning sensation.

He placed his attention on the road, gun empty. Yells and more shots were echoing faintly behind him, but he was well beyond accurate shooting range now and he had little to fear from that. Punching out the empty cartridges, he reloaded and jammed the pistol back into its holster. He then risked another look over his shoulder. Decket and the men were going into their saddles and starting to give chase. He smiled grimly. They'd get a run for their money, considering the start he had on them.

The borrowed buckskin was moving fast, fairly flying down the slight grade. The road was carved out of the mountain's slope, descending to the flats far below in a series of switchbacks and hairpin turns. At times sheer wall lifted on one side while abrupt, ragged cliffs dropped off for a hundred feet or more on the other.

He became aware gradually of the wound in his side as the anesthetic of shock wore thin with the passing seconds. It became a hot, stabbing pain and he turned to it, tearing his shirt angrily away when his fumbling fingers could not readily release the buttons. The place was a raw furrow bleeding freely. The bullet had just creased his ribs, tearing through the flesh but, luckily, breaking no bones. It was not dangerous but the steady loss of blood would do him no good.

A gunshot rang out, echoing loudly against the rock confines through which he was at that moment passing. He looked around. There were five riders behind him: Decket,

Perrick, the two men who had appeared to be deputies, and a new one. Santell gave him his close attention. He rode like an Indian, his legs flapping against the sides of his pony as he raced down the winding trail.

The road began to drop more sharply and Santell had an immediate worry about his next move. Soon he would reach the bottom of the long slope and break out onto the flats of the open prairie. He would then be an easy target for a man good with a rifle and he had little doubts there was such a marksman in the posse. And it was still hours until dark.

That would have to be the answer — darkness. If he could get off the road, turn into some canyon or deep wash and hide there until nightfall, his chances for getting away would improve a hundred per cent. But he would have to find a turnoff soon. He was rapidly approaching the end of the road, the foot of the slope. Already the pines and firs and tall blue spruce were thinning out, giving way to low and scrubby growth and bare rock.

He glanced again to Decket and the posse. They seemed closer but it could have been an illusion created by his own pressing anxiety. He searched along the way for that place into which he could swerve the buckskin and thus find sanctuary. At that moment they were rounding a wide curve, the back of which was perpendicular wall, the opposite side, sheer cliff falling away for a hundred or more feet. He pushed the buckskin for more speed, felt him respond. His hoofs were a steady drumming on the hard surface. And then, unaccountably, they seemed to be floating in space, soaring through the air with amazing smoothness. In the next instant Santell realized what had happened. The buckskin had stumbled.

He had a brief vision of the canyon lying before him, of the sky beyond the prairie, blue with a piling up of cottony clouds along the horizon. He wrenched himself from the saddle as the lip of the cliff rushed up. He plunged over the edge, clawing for a grasp on something, anything. He heard then the forlorn screams of the little buckskin.

In the next moment Santell struck heavily, crashing noisily into a clump of tough juniper. It dislodged a quantity of rock and loose gravel that went cascading off and downward. He bore the brunt of the impact upon his left shoulder and a sheet of white-hot flame flared through his injured side. He gasped as breath was wrenched from his lungs. Faintly, far, far below, he heard the buckskin again scream, fearfully, and then came the solid thud as he died on the rocks.

5

It was a matter of fleeting seconds, it seemed to Clay Santell, before Decket and his posse thundered by. They had not seen the unfortunate buckskin stumble and go over the edge, that scene being hidden from them by the curve. They assumed Santell was still somewhere ahead.

He crawled painfully from the prickling clutches of the juniper and dropped to a ledge a few feet below. His gun had been jarred from its holster and he had no idea where it had fallen. He could not recall hearing it strike in the rocks but he knew it was somewhere below, probably smashed and jammed beyond use. He lay on the ledge and searched the side of the cliff nevertheless. But the weapon was nowhere to be seen. Nor could he see the buckskin lying far below in the welter of brush and rock and a tremor passed through him as he thought about the pony. Had he been a second or two slower in hurling himself from the saddle, he would have been down there dead along with the game little horse.

His shoulder ached in unison with the

throb in his side where Decket's rifle bullet had grooved its course. But it was only wrenched and twisted and not broken, which again was a lucky thing for him. Something had to be done about the bleeding of his wound, however, and he turned to examining it again. The entire side of his undershirt was soaked with blood that oozed steadily from the puckered, raw flesh. Taking his bandana handkerchief, he ripped it into four strips and tied them together. Running this around his thick chest, he pulled it tight. It was a poor excuse for a bandage but it did seem to slow down the bleeding a little. Anyway, it would have to do for the time, until he could find better.

Where would that be?

The thought came suddenly to him. He was miles from Sutterville, the nearest town. And to return there would be nothing less than simply handing himself over to Decket. Being on foot now made plans for getting to Splendor, or any other settlement, a near impossibility. He gave the whole matter thorough consideration and could come to no good conclusion except for one thing — he could not remain where he was. Decket and the posse would come pounding back up the road in search of him just as soon as they reached the bottom of the slope and discovered he was not in front of them. They would guess him to be somewhere back along that last mile, below the curve they had seen him take.

They would hunt until they came to the place where the buckskin had tripped and then they would go down the side of the canyon and find the dead horse. And since he would not be there also lying dead, they would figure he had somehow escaped the fall and start beating the brush for him until they flushed him out, like some wild animal.

The critical urgency of the moment brought him to his feet. He stood there for a moment listening for sounds of the posse. There was nothing except the chatterings of a squirrel close by, but time had elapsed since they had swept past, so it could not be long before they came back. Even now they must be wheeling around.

He crawled stiffly off the ledge, surprised at the effort it took, and dropped to the almost straight up-and-down side of the canyon. It was a ten-foot drop and it sent a ragged flash of pain through him but he ignored it and moved on, crawling, sometimes walking upright when the going permitted it. He was doubling back. Such a course would take him away from where the buckskin had tripped, from the road itself, and while it offered no easy avenue for escape, leading as it did directly to the steep slope of another mountain, he at least would be some distance from where any search for him must originate.

The brush was thick and low, which helped. If he could reach a point a safe interval away he might hide while they had their look and then, when darkness fell, he could move on, assuming they had not discovered him.

He kept below the roadway, hurrying as best he could across the rough boulders and through the clutching brush. He reached a place where the road made its wide turn and hurried on. A heavy band of scrub oak lay across the apex shoulder of the curve and he burrowed into its depths, breathless and weary. It was then he heard the beat of the posse's horses coming up the road fast. He reached for his gun, remembering suddenly he no longer had one. Shrugging, he stretched out prone in the thick cover of bush and watched them draw near.

They might find him straight off. He considered that and was prepared for it. He would make a stand against them despite the odds, using his fists, rocks, a club — anything available. He had little to lose now, he reasoned. Eyes on the road, he watched them approach. Decket was in the lead, his face hard and set as frozen granite. Jake Perrick was close behind. He was followed by the other two deputies. The fifth rider drew his interest. He was an Indian, as he had suspected. He rode now along the edge of the cliff, keeping his gaze down as he looked for tell-tale signs.

Decket halted in the center of the curve and the others pulled up beside him. At that point they were all no farther than thirty feet distant. They turned to watch the Indian. He cruised slowly along, his brown face immobile as he made his close search.

"Travers has got to be along here somewheres," Decket said. "Someplace between here and the bottom of the hill. We saw him make this turn. Now, where did he go from here?"

"Ain't no place he could have turned off," Perrick said. "Cliff on one side and a wall a goat couldn't climb on the other."

"What's that Indian up to?" Decket said then, his voice ragged with impatience. "He sure has been little use to me so far!"

"Who knows what's in a redskin's head?" Jake Perrick murmured, drawing out his cigarette makings. "Looks like he might have found something, though," he added. He squinted at the Indian. "Hey, Charley!

You find him?"

The Indian glanced up. He wore a faded old army forage cap on his head and he pushed it to one side and scratched at his greasy black hair.

"Horse go here," he said in a flat tone.

"What?" Perrick demanded. "How the hell could a horse go off there? It's a hunnert feet to the bottom of that canyon!"

"Horse go here," Charley Ironhead repeated stolidly. "By damn!"

Decket muttered something beyond Santell's hearing and spurred his horse to the Indian's side. The others followed quickly. "What do you mean, horse go here?"

The Indian shrugged. "Horse jump. Maybe fall. Maybe him on bottom. Dead."

"Maybe the devil!" Perrick exclaimed, coming off his saddle and walking to the edge of the cliff. "If that horse jumped off here, he's plenty dead. And so's the man that was riding him!"

Santell watched the satisfaction spread across Decket's pinched face. The relief was plain and he knew then he was right about the lawman's plans for him. His breath tightened in his throat in that next moment. Charley Ironhead, standing in the midst of the four men, was staring straight at him. Or at the spot where he lay hidden. The

Indian's black, obsidian bright eyes were unblinking, drilling into the oak brush relentlessly. Santell dared not move, fearing the slightest thing would give him away.

"Well, he sure never jumped a purpose," Perrick declared then, looking down into the canyon. "Maybe he stumbled coming around that bend. You think he stumbled, Charley?"

The Indian dropped his glance and began a slow inspection of the rocks in the road. Santell took a deep, full breath. He was still not sure if the Indian actually suspected he was hidden there or was merely staring into space while he nursed his thoughts. He watched Charley Ironhead as he moved about. They would know what had taken place in a minute now. After covering a small area, the Indian straightened up and pointed to one of the larger stones thrusting up from the road's surface. Perrick bent over to examine it closely.

"Sure has got a shiny spot on it," he announced. "Like maybe a horseshoe hit against it. Reckon that's your answer, Mr. Decket," he added, swiveling back to the marshal. "The horse stumbled on that rock and pitched them over the cliff, your Shotgun Travers and all. Two bits says they're both dead, horse and man, down there on the bottom."

"Could be," Decket said. "However, I've got to see him. And I'll need your sworn verification. Let's go find him."

"Won't be hard to do," Perrick said cheerfully. "He ought to be layin' right with the horse." He turned to the Indian. "Take a look, Charley. See if they ain't both down there, deader'n a plugged buzzard."

The Indian trotted to the edge of the road, cast about momentarily for the best route and then leaped to a rock a dozen or so feet below. He paused there for a time searching the brushy depths with infinite care. Apparently finding nothing and not satisfied with his position, he dropped lower to another ledge.

"There horse," he called up immediately.

"See the man?" Perrick yelled back.

"See horse. No man."

"Well, he's down there somewhere," Perrick grumbled. "Maybe a little over to one side." He glanced to Harry Decket. "Reckon we all better go down and have a look. He sure couldn't have got no place else."

A flame of hope leaped into life in Clay Santell. If they all went down into the canyon leaving their horses unattended on the road, he could slip out and quietly borrow one. A moment later that hope died.

Decket, never gambling where his own interests were concerned, dismounted slowly. "Good idea. But leave a man up here with these horses, Jake. Could be Travers is around somewhere just looking for a chance to get another horse. Could just be he's not down there."

Perrick threw the marshal a baffled look. "How you figure that? He's got to be down there!"

Decket said, "I don't *know* he's down there dead. I figure he is but until I see him, I don't bank on anything for certain."

"Stay with the horses, Tex," Perrick said.

"One thing more," the marshal continued. "I'm not of a mind to mess around with this jasper any longer. Don't waste time on questions if he's still alive. Shoot him."

"Thought you was so set on taking him alive," Perrick reminded.

"Your name on his death certificate will be good enough for me now. I've had all the trouble with this Travers I can swallow. Makes no difference to Colorado, anyway."

"Whatever you say, Mr. Decket," Perrick murmured. "You hear him, boys? You see Travers, shoot to kill."

"I heard," the man called Tex replied.

"Me, too," the older deputy added.

The Indian was already making his way

down the slope. Santell watched as the others went over the edge after him, dislodging stones that clattered noisily. His hopes soared again. If they all got down there except the redhead, Tex, he might still have a chance of getting one of the horses. The man sat at the lip of the cliff, his back partly turned to Santell as he watched the activity of the rest of the posse. If he could manage to creep upon Tex quietly enough. . . .

"Might be a good idea for me to stay along about here," Jake Perrick pointed out, coming to a halt upon a ledge a few feet below the crown of the road. "I can watch the brush ahead of you fellers. If he tries to scoot out ahead of you, I can pot him from here."

"Good idea," Decket said with a complimentary wave of his hand and continued on downward.

Santell cursed bitterly under his breath. Another chance gone. With only Tex to contend with he might have pulled it off but with Perrick remaining where he was, it was out of the question. He would be caught between a crossfire and, with the instructions Harry Decket had given, he would be a dead man in less than ten feet.

Shoot to kill — on sight!

The full meaning of that drove into his

consciousness fully for the first time. He was now a hunted man without even the hope of surrender. His only hope was to get where he was known, where he could prove he was not an outlaw named Shotgun Travers, and the nearest point where that could be done was miles away. How, then, could he get there?

He lay back, tired, while a feeling of desperation pushed slowly through him. He could no longer see Decket or the Indian or the other deputy. They were now too far below the surface to be visible. Tex sat on his stony perch and Jake Perrick's large bulk was half in view on the shelf he had chosen to guard.

Santell was becoming a little lightheaded from the loss of blood and his shoulder was growing stiffer by the moment from the blow it had taken in the fall. He became increasingly aware that it was not safe to remain where he lay for much longer. He had to do something and do it soon. When they failed to find him at the bottom of the canyon with the buckskin, they would put the Indian to ferreting out his trail. And the Indian would find it, there was no doubt of that. Charley Ironhead, he suspected, already had some ideas about where he might be.

He twisted about, looking into the country that lay behind him. It was a long mountainside, brushy, rough, and it would be slow going. But it was the only course left open and unguarded to him. Mustering his strength, he moved with extreme slowness and caution so as to not dislodge any rocks or rattle the dry brush, and wormed his way out of the oak thicket. He had to get as much distance as possible between himself and the road before Charley Ironhead started looking for him. When he reached a point where he could no longer see Tex or Jake Perrick, he got to his feet and started running.

He heard a faint yell and his heart skipped a beat, thinking he had been discovered. Perrick made some sort of reply to the cry but he was too far away to distinguish the words. He suspected they had discovered he was not at the bottom of the canyon. He did not pause but hurried on, pressed by the necessity to get as far from Decket and the posse as possible. He was using no caution now, plunging on recklessly, ignoring the pain in his shoulder and side, a man in full, desperate flight. . . .

It was beginning to grow darker in the forest. He noticed this when finally, spent and weak, he had to rest. Soon it would be night and that would be of much help to him; Charley Ironhead could do no tracking then and would have to wait until daylight. But that would not stop them entirely. Decket would continue to hunt for him, riding the slopes and canyons, not waiting nor depending entirely upon the Indian.

He rested five short minutes, shaking his head periodically to clear the mist that persisted in gathering in his eyes. He wished he had a drink — whisky, water, coffee, just anything liquid; he didn't really care what it was just so it would allay the terrible dryness in his throat. He got to his feet and started off again, the down grade offering him his one advantage. He had given no thought to where he was going, nor to where the course he had taken would eventually lead. He was past caring about that. The important thing was to escape from Harry Decket and the man's calculated determination to kill him.

Escape Decket and somehow reach Hall McGivern in Splendor. That became the paramount thing in his mind, his only hope. But McGivern was days away, on the far side of miles and miles of open plains country. And Santell was a man on foot with no supplies of any sort. It was a hopeless situation and he knew it. But it was not in his makeup to give up.

A rabbit skittered out from beneath his feet. Bright alarm flooded through him. He stumbled to a halt, clawing for the gun at his hip that wasn't there. Then he realized it was no more than a rabbit, fleeing for its life even as was he.

He moved on, weaving a little on his feet, falling once or twice as exposed roots tripped him up. He was punishing himself cruelly in his haste to get somewhere, anywhere beyond the reach of Decket and the posse.

He came to a sudden halt. The faint smell of wood smoke touched his nostrils. He drew himself up, straining, sniffling the closing darkness. It was coming from downwind, on the breeze off the prairie. A small sound escaped his throat and he plunged eagerly on through the night.

6

In a narrow, cut-back canyon a short two miles below the point where the Sutterville road broke out of the mountains and onto the plains, Melissa York made her night camp. She had driven the team and canvas-topped spring wagon as deeply as possible into the slash in order that the fire would not be seen by any travelers. She wanted no visitors, having small trust in men or this violent land that had taken everything, including her father and brother, from her.

It was not yet dark, a time of day she ordinarily would enjoy when the day's heat began to dwindle and the sky would be flooded with bright color and the creatures of the wild preparing themselves with much chattering for the coming night. But there was no joy or comfort in it for her now. It was to be her first night alone on the long road back to Missouri, and she was unsure of her own courage.

She unhitched the team and picketed them on the good grass at the end of the canyon, looking very much like a small boy, dressed as she was in her brother's old clothing. She drew a bucket of water from the wooden cask in the rear of the wagon and placed it where the horses could get at it easily and then set about gathering a supply of firewood. She paused now and then to listen, to glance along the mountain slope or out at the prairie, not looking for any one thing or person but watching as a lonely, frightened woman will. She could not account for her feelings but something nagged at her persistently, turning her edgy and nervous.

When she had enough wood to satisfy her collected and piled under the wagon to keep dry in case of rain, she built a small fire for cooking purposes. After it was well started, she climbed into the wagon seat, pausing there beside the straw dummy she had rigged up in her father's clothing. She had carefully tied it to the forward upright in as natural a position as she could contrive, believing that passersby, at a reasonable distance at least, would look and behold not a young and extremely pretty girl making her way across the prairie alone but two men, one young and one much older.

From the depths of the canvas shroud she procured her father's old single-barrel scattergun and laid it across the floorboards where it would be handy. She then opened the warchest and selected what food she would use for the evening meal, obtained the necessary pots and pans, and returned to the fire. She set about at once to prepare her solitary meal, feeling the loneliness intensely. The supper was simple and soon ready: coffee, a broth made of boiling a chunk of dried beef in seasoned, thickened water, and warmed-over biscuits she had made the day before at the mine.

Sitting near the fire, sipping her cup of coffee, she listened to the steady cropping of the horses as they grazed and to the distant calls of nightbirds. Her father had always loved this time of day, too, finding much beauty in all things wild, in the hush of sunsets and glowing sunrises. But that had really been one of his shortcomings. She realized that now. He had always been too much of a dreamer to be practical.

Her cup was empty and she refilled it again from the simmering pot resting above the flames. The day had been long and she was tired. It had not been a particularly good one insofar as traveling was concerned. She had covered less than fifteen miles since dawn. But, she comforted herself, that was because she had been forced to swing wide of Sutterville to avoid running into Jake Perrick.

After her father had died as the result of an unexplainable cave-in at their small mine shaft, Perrick had made several calls upon her, always with the same evil purpose in mind. She was a lone woman in a vast wilderness of silence and he considered her fair game. The last time he had come she had rid herself of him only by threatening him with the scattergun, realizing in those moments the future there held no peace for her. That was when she decided to fullfill her promise to her father as he lay breathing his last: she would forget the mine, she would leave the country. She would take their few, pitiful belongings and go back to Missouri where there were relatives. The empty, silent hills of Colorado were no place for a twenty-one-year-old girl completely alone.

She had been fortunate that first day, she had to admit. She had met no one and so the trip from the mine shack to this spot in the canyon on the edge of the prairie had been uneventful. Tomorrow, however, she could not hope for such good luck. There were bound to be others traveling who would want to be friendly, who would want to stop and pass the time of day with an out-bound pilgrim. Well, she would do her best to avoid them. The longer she could fool others into believing she was a man and that her father rode on the seat beside her, the better off she would be. It came suddenly to her that her fear and hate for Jake Perrick had wrought a vast change in her; it had engendered a powerful mistrust of all men.

The fire was dying and she tossed a few more dry branches into it. She checked the water bucket placed before the horses and finding it empty, refilled it. She came back to the lifting flames and stood there staring into their flickering depths, rummaging through her mind for any details, any little chores left undone and that should be accomplished before she turned in for the night. She was standing there, like that, in deep study, when she heard the first alarming sounds in the nearby brush.

A gush of panic raced through her but she choked back any outcry. Taking a firm grasp of her nerves, she pivoted slowly about to the wagon and took up the scattergun. She rested it upon the top of the vehicle's front wheel and waited. The fire was now burning brightly and she was thankful for its flaring fan of light, which afforded her a good view of the immediate area surrounding her camp.

The brush rattled again, loudly, as if it might be a horse in trouble, floundering about to stay on its feet. But what would a horse be doing running loose on the steep side of the mountain? So she waited, calm now, ready for anything. And then quite suddenly a man was standing in the ring of yellow light.

He came from the confusion of rock and brush and halted. He was breathing heavily and his face was distorted from the effort of breaking through the difficult terrain. He wore a wide-brimmed cattleman's hat although the rest of his clothing was common enough to the country. A gunbelt encircled his waist but she saw no gun in the holster slung at his hip.

Melissa's first thoughts were that it was one of Jake Perrick's men, that he had discovered her departure and was searching the country for her, knowing she could not have gone far. But a moment later she dismissed that; a man of Perrick's would be mounted, not clambering about the slope in the dark. No, this fellow would be someone else; a man lost in the night. Or an outlaw on the run. A small chill moved through her.

She saw him lift his eyes to the dummy, indefinite in the shadows beyond the firelight, and was thankful she had thought to take that precaution. Taking a firm hold on her voice, she wagged the scattergun at the intruder and said, "What do you want?"

The man flicked another glance at the dummy on the wagon seat. "You folks heading east, ma'am?"

She realized her own disguise had fooled him not at all, even in the half-darkness, and it angered her. Tomorrow she would start wearing that old pair of bib overalls that had been her father's. They would be baggy enough to conceal her figure.

"Why?" she asked guardedly.

"Lost my horse," he said, breathing more regularly now. "Have to get to Texas, to a town just across the line. Sure would appreciate your letting me ride with you."

He was an outlaw then. Everybody said Texas was a haven for outlaws and criminals endeavoring to escape the laws of other states and territories. She looked him over carefully. He didn't have the face of a criminal. He was big, too, and not very old. Maybe twenty-four or five. And good-looking, she decided, in a husky, powerful sort of way. His shoulders were the broadest she had ever seen and there was a look of untested strength to him tempered by a sort of polite gentleness. He would be a good one to have along on the trip to Missouri; any man, including Jake Perrick, would think twice before tangling with him. But that was all foolish thinking; why should he be any different than Jake Perrick or any other man?

She raised her eyes to him. He was regarding her with a patient sort of smile on his lips. She said, "Sorry, but we've got no room. You'll have to find yourself another way to get to Texas."

"I could help drive," he suggested. "And should you break down, I'm right handy at repairs."

It was a good point, one that had worried her no end when she had first planned the trip. What would she do if she broke an axle or a wheel? But she was a woman alone with little defense and no trust at all where men were concerned. In a voice suddenly brittle, she said, "Get out! You'll find no help here," and waggled the scattergun at him.

He shrugged his thick shoulders. "Yes, ma'am. Just give me a minute to get my breath clear back." He moved in closer to the fire, ignoring the threat of the shotgun, and sat down upon a flat boulder. Removing his hat he wiped away the sweat from his forehead with a wrist. "Could you spare me a drink of water?"

Melissa regarded him warily, making no reply. He grinned at her. "Lay down your gun, ma'am. I'll not do you any harm."

She studied him for another moment and then turned and laid the gun across the dummy's lap, making a great show of it. She murmured, "Watch him," in a voice calculated to reach his ears and then moved on to the back of the wagon. She filled the tin dipper and wheeled back to take it to him. She found he had left the rock and was standing next to the fire. Eyeing her soberly, he accepted the dipper, thanked her and tipped it to his lips.

He was wounded. She saw it when he half-turned from her. His shirt was ragged and torn, stained with blood. A makeshift bandage circled his chest. In a matter-of-fact tone she said, "You've been shot."

"Nothing bad," he murmured. He was looking down at the pot of coffee warming over the fire.

She saw his interest and said, "Help yourself. But soon as you've had your fill, you'll have to move on along."

He gave her a broad smile and dropped to his heels, hunkering near the flames as she had so often seen her father do. He filled the dipper with coffee and drank it down, enjoying it fully.

"Mighty good," he observed. "Not many women can make good coffee. Always too stingy with the grounds, I reckon."

He got to his feet, rising to his full height. "I'm much obliged to you. Now, I'll be getting along."

On sudden impulse Melissa said, "Better let me take a look at that wound before you go. You won't get far with it bleeding like it is."

"It's all right," he replied quickly, almost harshly, some sort of suspicion seemingly to move through him.

She ignored it and made her inspection. When she was finished she stepped back. "Who shot you?"

"The marshal. Fellow name of Decket who I ran across in your town of Sutterville."

"Not my town," she flared back. Then, "Decket. I never heard of him before. The sheriff's name is Wilhelm."

"Decket's a U.S. marshal. I don't know where he's from."

She studied him for a full minute. "Then you're an outlaw. You're wanted by the law?"

"Not that I know of, except for this. Decket claims I am. Says I was his prisoner and that I escaped from him. Now they're all trying to get their hands on me. Fact is, I'm nobody's prisoner. Never was. I was just passing through the town when this marshal spotted me."

"But I don't understand. Can't you prove you're not the man who escaped him?"

"Nobody around here who knows me or who can back me up. Closest friend I've got is in Texas. That's why I'm trying to get there before they catch up to me. Only chance I've got to clear my name."

"You won't get anywhere unless that wound is patched up," Melissa stated flatly. "Take off that shirt while I heat some water

77

and get bandages."

She dumped the remaining broth onto the ground and refilled the pot with clean water. Santell removed his wool shirt and then the bloody undergarment, which he tossed into the brush. He tried to take off the improvised bandage but it was stuck tight to the wound. He left it for her, feeling much better now with the hot coffee inside his belly.

Melissa returned to the fire where the water was beginning to boil, bringing with her a strip of white cloth and a bottle of some sort of medicine. She placed the bottle on the ground and began to rip the cloth into narrow widths. Santell was having his first good look at her. She had black hair and her eyes, ordinarily blue, were almost jet in the firelight's glow. She was lightly tanned and had a spray of freckles across her nose. The loosely-fitting man's garb, outlandish and bulky, failed entirely to hide her womanly attributes.

She felt the push of his gaze and without looking up said, "Don't get any ideas about me changing my mind, Mr. — Mr. —"

"Santell. Clay Santell."

"Mr. Santell. I'm Melissa York. I'd do as much for a dog or a horse that had been hurt. Soon as I get you fixed up, you'll be on your way."

78

"Sure," he said. Then, "Don't figure that's such a good idea, you being out here alone like this. Reckon that straw man of yours won't fool many people."

There was a dry humor in his tone and she felt a rush of dismay at his discovery. Keeping her hands still to hide their trembling she said, "At a hundred yards it will serve the purpose. I don't aim to let anybody get any closer than that."

"I'll be glad to come along —" he began.

She sliced through his words coldly. "No, thank you."

He was silent for a long space of time after that, standing there by the fire, his gaze reaching out to the felt black prairie. The pot began to boil and she set it aside. Folding one of the strips into a pad she dipped it into the scalding water and motioned for him to raise his arm. He did so and she held the pad against the wound, softening the hard crust that bound the old bandage to the raw flesh.

"I don't think you have much trust in men," he murmured.

"Only two I ever did, my father and brother, are both dead."

"I see. You mentioned the sheriff of Sutterville — Wilhelm, or whatever his name is. If he's the sheriff, who is Jake Perrick?"

She stepped quickly away from him, her eyes sparking angrily. "What about Jake Perrick?"

"He's one of the posse helping the marshal. The head man of it, looks like. Why? He a friend of yours?"

"He is no friend of mine!" she declared, her face flushing hotly. "He never was! I — I hate him! He killed my brother. I'm sure of it. Put a bullet in his back one day when he was riding to town. And he had something to do with the accident that caused my father's death. I don't know just what but he had a hand in it. If ever I get a good chance, I'll kill Jake Perrick!"

Santell waited for the fierce outburst to ebb, for the wild storm in her eyes to pass. Then he said, "Why would he do all that? He got something against your family?"

"You really are a stranger around here," she said, contritely. "Everybody knows Jake is the hired killer for the King Midas Syndicate. Oh, his official title is Land Superintendent or something like that, but it's just a cover-up for his real job. They wanted our claim but we were all filed on it legally and there was nothing they could do about it. They tried to buy my father out but he thought the mine was a good one and wouldn't sell."

She paused to probe at the bandage again, loosening it gently with her fingertips.

"He wouldn't sell?"

"No. So they put Jake Perrick on the job."

"And he got the job done."

"Yes!" she said, savagely and ripped the bandana bandage from the wound in a single, sweeping motion.

Santell jumped and an oath escaped his lips. He frowned at her.

"I'm sorry," she apologized at once, giving him a smile. Making a fresh pad, she wet it and set to cleaning out the ugly, raw furrow, working at it with care. "I left soon after my father was buried. Perrick seemed to think I was his private property then. He kept dropping by at all hours, day and night. Every time I looked around, it seemed, there he was, grinning and talking in that filthy way of his."

The wound was finally cleansed to her satisfaction and she made a third pad, soaking it well in the medicine from the bottle. Bidding him to hold the square of cloth in place, she fashioned a lengthy bandage, drew it around his chest and pulled it tight. She was very close to him in those moments, her arms almost encircling him, her dark hair brushing against his rough cheek.

It was a disturbing feeling to Santell. It

had been a long time since a woman had been so close. A long time since Eva. His thoughts cooled at once, thinking then of her. He shifted his eyes from Melissa's serene, tanned face to the darkness beyond the clearing. She had no trust in men; she had told him so and she showed it in the way she rebuffed him. It was a thing he could understand for there was little trust in him for any woman, either.

The wound began to smart like fire as the medicine took effect. She finished placing the bandage and fell back a step, regarding him intently. It was almost as if she had expected him to seize her and crush her in his powerful arms, taking advantage when she was close, and now she was having a difficult time understanding why he had not.

"I'm obliged again," he said, "I'll be moving on." He sobered. "Hope my coming here won't cause you trouble from the posse — from Jake Perrick. They get to trailing me, they'll come right to your camp."

"Are they hunting you now, tonight?"

"I figure they are. The marshal's not going to give it up easy. Right now they're probably combing out the draws and working the slope. They've got that Indian tracker with them."

"Even an Indian could do little good in

the dark."

"I know that but they can all keep moving and looking. You best be on your guard."

She met his eyes across the failing camp-fire, question and indecision filling her with a light worry. "I wonder —" she began to frame a question and then stopped short.

Santell's keen hearing had caught up the sound also. The slow, spaced footfalls of an approaching horse. He stepped forward quickly and snatched up the scattergun. Wheeling, he backed out of the fan of the fire's glow, fading into the deep shadows behind the wagon.

"Don't be afraid," he said softly. "I'll be right here with you until we know who it is."

7

In the solid shadows of a low-spreading cedar Clay Santell waited. Melissa, like a startled bird, remained caught up in the flaring, flickering light of the fire as the sounds of the approaching horseman drew nearer.

Three men, not just one, rode into the camp. It was Jake Perrick, the redheaded deputy they called Tex, and the older man. Decket and the Indian were not with them and he guessed the party had split in order that more territory could be covered. The riders pulled to a halt in front of the girl, Perrick showed first surprise on his moon-like face and then a strong, glittering-eyed interest.

"Well! Well! If it ain't the uppity little filly from the mine! And all by her lonesome. Now, what you doing way off here in the dark, honey?"

Perrick's shifting eyes swept the wagon, noting its load of household goods and personal belongings. "Why, I do believe you're trying to leave us! And without so much as a by-your-leave. Now, you know that wouldn't be right, honey — runnin' off without telling old Jake goodbye."

Perrick came slowly off the saddle and handed the reins to Tex. The girl, watching intently with wide eyes, began to back toward the wagon. Perrick laughed, a coarse, guttural sound in the night.

"What's the matter, honey? You don't need to be afraid of nothin', not with old Jake around to keep you company." He paused there, throwing his glance about the camp. "You ain't had no other visitor, have you? A big man, walking?"

Melissa York found her voice. She said, "Get out of here, Jake Perrick! Get out!"

The big man turned to her in mock surprise. "Now, that ain't very hospitable," he rumbled chidingly. "Me and the boys has had a hard day. And it's a right smart ride back to town. I just figured we'd spend the night right here with you. This is a real cozy camp."

"Get out!" Melissa repeated in a low, tense voice.

Perrick looked her up and down with cool anticipation. "I reckon not, honey. I been waiting a long time for this."

Santell saw her throw an involuntary, frightened look toward him. Perrick's attention immediately swiveled to that point and he had a moment during which he set himself for trouble. But after a time the thick-bodied Perrick, thinking of other things, came back to his two companions.

"Supposing you two meander over there near those rocks and rest your bones a spell. The marshal and the redskin will be along directly. And while we're just waitin', the little filly and me has got some unfinished business to take care of. When that's done, I'll see if I can talk her into stirrin' us up a bite of supper."

Tex grunted and said, "Come on, Sam," and immediately pulled out of the camp, pointing for a hollow some fifty or sixty yards away. Melissa began to retreat quietly as Perrick watched his men depart. She moved along the wagon, following out its tongue, circling it. Perrick, satisfied the men were out of hearing, clasped his hands together and rubbed the palms tightly. He turned his attention back to the girl.

He chuckled, seeing she had moved. "Hey, now! That's sure no way to act! Old Jake likes his women lively but not skittish."

He moved after her, fast on his feet for so big a man. The light of the dwindling fire played against his bulky shape and laid an oily shine across his sweaty, broad face. The rancid odor of him was like some evil cloud.

Melissa continued to ease away, her face still, her lips compressed to a firm line. Santell watched her draw nearer. This would have to be quick and it would have to be quiet. He threw a glance across the dim, starlit distance to where Tex and Sam had halted. As he looked a small flame broke the night and a campfire burst into life, blackly outlining the two men.

"One thing you're goin' to learn," Perrick's deep voice rumbled, "is that it sure don't pay to get uppity with old Jake. And there's sure no use runnin'. You ain't going no place, not this night."

The man was little more than a yard away.

The rasp of his spurred breathing was plain. Santell stepped from the shadows and hit him with all his strength. The blow was like the drive of a locomotive piston, landing squarely on Perrick's stubbled chin. His head snapped back and he dropped without a sound. For a fraction of time Santell thought he had broken the man's neck and he cared little. At his elbow Melissa gave a sigh of relief. He turned to her.

"There's no staying here now for either of us. The marshal and the Indian will be along any time, and besides, Tex and Sam will get suspicious after a while. Best thing we can do is hitch up and move on. You get the team in harness while I truss up Perrick. Watch the noise — sound will carry on a night like this."

"All right," she replied softly and hurried off.

He was having quick, admiring thoughts of this Melissa York. There had been no frantic, womanly hysteria in her manner when Perrick and the others rode in. She had been frightened but she coolly led the lawman around the wagon into Santell's reach. She had made no outcry when he smashed the man to the ground. And when he had directed her to quietly and quickly assemble the team she had done so without asking any questions.

A real woman, this Melissa York. A twinge of regret passed through him then; regret that he had brought this trouble to her. If Perrick and the others had not been searching for him they likely would never have stumbled into her camp. But if it had to be this way, he was glad he was with her when Perrick showed up. A shudder passed through him when he thought of her slim body in the crushing hands of the big man.

He wheeled then to the wagon. Taking up the remainder of the white cloth left over from the bandages and finding a short length of rope, he first gagged the still-unconscious Perrick. With the stout manila, he bound his hands behind, looped them to the feet and dragged the heavy figure into the brush. Then he went to help Melissa.

The hitching up was almost finished and he completed it for her, moving swiftly and silently with the harness. When that was done, he took her by the waist and swung her lightly onto the seat.

Remembering his lost gun, he moved back to Perrick's quiet shape and plucked the pistol from the scabbard and thrust it into his own. He returned to her.

"I'll walk ahead," he said in a low voice. "It's a fairly dark night and with a little luck we can get miles away from here before they find out what's happened."

"Wouldn't it be faster if you drove?"

He shook his head. "Can't take a chance on a wheel banging up against a rock and raising a racket. I'll lead; I can pick the way for the horses."

She said no more but settled herself alongside the dummy. She had the old scattergun across her lap and it reminded Santell of pictures of pioneer women who rode their huge Conestogas through Indian country, prepared to fight if need be for their lives and their family.

He moved to the head of the team and took the off-horse by the headstall. Glancing upward he noted the heavy clouds that had begun to collect shortly before sundown were closely but steadily blotting out the stars. It would be both a help and a hindrance; an overcast would provide a dark shroud to mask their traveling but also made for a dangerous and difficult trail.

He swung the wagon about in a tight circle, walking a step ahead of the horses, carefully avoiding the rocks lying in the draw and keeping to the loose sand. The vehicle groaned and creaked and the harness jingled alarmingly, it seemed to Santell. But it could not be done more quietly.

He chose a course that carried them away from the dozing deputies. This was taking them toward the road, a direction he did not wish to follow, but it was necessary they swing wide of the men. When he figured they were far enough away not to be heard, he would alter the route and curve back southward. This would place them along a band of brush and scrubby growth that edged out onto the plains from the mountain and would conceal their movements.

But would safety lie there?

The wagon's tracks would be plain to see on the prairie. Anybody would be able to follow them, there'd be no need for Charley Ironhead, the Indian. And as soon as daylight came, possibly sooner, they would all be on the trail, Decket thirsting for his blood, Perrick after Melissa York. One thing was certain, the farther away they were before the posse got onto those tracks, the better off they would be. They reached the end of the canyon and broke out onto the flat land. There actually would be less danger here now insofar as noise was concerned; there were fewer rocks to contend with, only an occasional upthrusting of stone not yet covered by the wind's shifting of loose sand or the spring torrents that raged down from the high mountains.

Santell left his position in front of the team and climbed up beside Melissa. He glanced to his right, to a winking spot of fire on the slope. He could barely make out the two hunched figures crouched around the small flame. They had not yet become suspicious.

"So far, so good," Santell commented, taking up the reins. He clucked the team into a slow trot. "A few hundred yards more and we'll be on the safe side, at least until daylight."

"What happens then?" Melissa asked quietly.

He shook his head. "Hard to say. They'll find our wagon tracks, that's a sure thing. Might be a good idea for me to leave you before then. They won't stop to bother you if I'm not around."

She waited out a full minute. Somewhere, in the distance, thunder rolled. Then, "You don't know Jake Perrick," she said with a hopeless shrug. "I've never been afraid before of anything — or any man. He is the exception."

"Decket won't let him bother you. He's too anxious to get his claws on me. He'll keep Jake on that job."

She shook her head. "Jake would fix it so the marshal would never know. He would make out like he was hunting you but instead he would slip off and circle back until he found me. I know. And Decket wouldn't be any the wiser. Tex London and that other deputy, Sam Cunningham, wouldn't say anything about it."

"I see," Santell murmured. "We've got a mighty poor chance for escape. This wagon leaves big tracks."

He looked back again at the distant campfire. They were almost directly opposite it at that moment and it showed up larger and much brighter. One of the deputies was throwing more fuel into it.

"I was thinking of that," Melissa said. "There are two saddles in the back, my brother's and my own. Why not drive the wagon as far as we can and then hide it? We could unharness the team and throw the saddles on them and make a run for it. We'd make better time."

"That would be leaving all your things — losing all your belongings."

"Better to do that than have that posse catch up with us."

He nodded soberly. But he was having his own deep thoughts about it. He was wishing again he had not blundered into Melissa York's camp. It complicated things for him, placing a greater necessity for his own survival. Alone, he could slip in and out of hiding, move by night if necessary; and if it came to a final, critical point when he no longer felt he could run, he could stand and make a fight of it; he had a gun now, Jake Perrick's. But having her with him, actually in his care, ruled all that out. She was depending solely upon him.

Women and trouble — they were a single package, it seemed to him. It was only the trouble that varied. With Eva it had been one kind; with this Melissa York it was another. He had said once he was through with such things, that never again would any woman draw him into a position where he was near helpless. But here he was once more, caught again, trapped between a rock and a hard place, unable to do his own wishes.

A trace of impatience in his voice, he said, "Isn't there a ranch house or some home-steader around somewhere where you could go and be safe?"

"Not for sixty miles or more. All there is near here is an old abandoned way station where the stage coaches used to stop years ago. They haven't used it for a long time." She hesitated, the edge of his tone having revealed to her some of his thinking. "I'm sorry that I'm in your way. By yourself you'd have a good chance for getting away from Decket, of reaching your friend in Texas and clearing your name."

Santell did not face her, feeling a strong measure of shame and embarrassment at having his thoughts read. "You forget I'm on foot. A man can't go far in this country without a horse."

"But you could hide out. Find a good place in the hills and keep out of sight for a time."

"Remember Charley Ironhead; that's what he's along for, to track me down if I try that."

He looked again toward the camp of the deputies. Both men were standing near the flames, their figures outlined blackly against the flaring light. Another quarter mile and the wagon would be outside their view, a few minutes more and they would drop behind a roll of hills and be out of sight. Thunder murmured distantly again, far to the north along the rim of mountains. The swiftly scudding clouds would soon have the sky shut away. That would be welcome.

"We'll hide the wagon as soon as you think it's safe to stop," Melissa said then, coming to a decision. "We'll use the saddles and ride until we reach some place where I can stay. You can go on. Without me. You're welcome to one of the horses."

He considered her words, turned silent by her sacrifice. She had realized she was a burden upon his shoulders and now she was trying to rectify that. He said, "I don't know about that, about leaving you. I'm not sure it would be a smart idea."

"It's what I want, Clay."

He shook his head. "Just where would this safe place be you mentioned? You've already said there wasn't one within sixty miles or so."

Melissa started to make her answer. A gunshot crashed through the darkness, coming from the canyon where she had pitched her camp a few hours before. Jake Perrick had got free of his bonds somehow and had raised the alarm. Watching the campfire, Santell saw the two figures suddenly disappear.

He reached for the whip and said, his face grim, "Our luck just ran out, lady."

8

A long mile to the north came an answering shot. Marshal Harry Decket and the Indian. They had heard Perrick's summons and were making a reply — a prearranged signal, no doubt.

Now the chase had begun in earnest, he thought. Now they were on his trail, one they would close in on quickly and relentlessly until he was finally run to bay or else reached Splendor where he could prove he was not a man Harry Decket needed to kill. And Perrick would have Melissa.

He popped the whip over the team's backs and they lunged forward in the harness. Pans and boxes in the wagon-bed began to clatter and slam about as the vehicle increased its speed down the long slope. A bullet ripped through the canvas, which, Santell suddenly realized, was a perfect target looming up ghostly white in the darkness.

"Down on the floor!" he yelled to Melissa.

She complied at once, dropping to her knees in front of the seat. Santell, half standing, crouched like a man driving a racing chariot and laid the whip to the flying team. They were running full tilt, near wild flight, surging down the hillside with the wagon crowding at their heels.

Another gun cracked, the report yet distant and hollow. Santell never saw where the shot came from nor heard it pass. Behind them, he guessed. He was straining to see ahead, to locate the occasional rocks that pushed up through the soil or the narrow, deep washes that drained the hills and could break a horse's leg or toss a speeding wagon into a splintering wreck. Despite the thickening overcast the canvas cover of the wagon was a dead giveaway and the sooner they reached the trees and pulled deep into their screen of foliage, the safer they would be.

But that was far ahead, a mile or so to where a darker blur in the night marked the stand of brush and trees. They were too distant for him to tell exactly what the cover would be but he knew it would provide them with some degree of safety.

"Hang on to the dashboard!" he yelled to Melissa. "We'll try to make that brush over there!"

He saw her look ahead, beyond the team's laboring bodies. "Can we make it in time?"

"Anybody's guess. We'll sure give it a try!"

There had been no more shooting, at least during the last few minutes and this, paradoxically, worried him. It could mean Perrick and his deputies had decided the range was too great. What, then, were they doing? Waiting for Decket and Charley Ironhead or were they slicing across the flats intending to intercept them before they could reach the shelter of the trees? Maybe they did not plan to shoot at all, secure in the knowledge that there really was no escape ahead for Melissa and Santell, that it was just a matter of time before they overtook and captured them both.

He risked a glance over his right shoulder. His jaw came shut with a snap and settled into a hard line. That was just what they were doing. Three riders were bearing down upon them, sweeping in at an angle designed to bring them in ahead. Santell swung back to the team. They were doing their best but he called upon them for more.

The wagon was swaying dangerously, not constructed for such high-speed traveling. They had been fortunate so far. The wild ride down the slope was over smooth terrain. He had been able to swing clear of the rock piles and the arroyos had been gentle, no more than shallow, slope-walled washes. Lucky, too lucky, he thought. But the dark blur of the brush was nearer. He headed the team directly for it, throwing them into a gradual climb as they looped back toward the mountain.

A gun barked, uncomfortably close. The bullet dug sod a few yards ahead of the straining horses. Perrick had spotted the move and was trying to close them off. A spatter of bullets came then, lacing through the darkness, all of them close but deliberately missing their target. Santell lashed at the team, driving it hard. The band of trees rushed up, now no more than fifty yards away. And then Melissa cried out.

"Santell!"

A narrow, square-edged arroyo loomed suddenly before them. Instinctively the horses leaped, clearing it. The front wheels of the wagon struck hard, dropped solidly. The vehicle seemed to buckle in the center as the back end flew up, going high into the air, and, started over.

"Jump!" Santell yelled.

Melissa leaped clear. Santell was not long behind her. The wagon crashed to one side, its hoops collapsing as it bounced and came down hard on the canvas sheeting. Cans, boxes, tools, clothing and an assortment of other items spewed about in the night as if tossed by an explosion.

"The trees!" Santell shouted as he met the ground, went into a full-length sprawl and rolled back to his feet. "Run for it!"

He started for the dark stand of shadows, pulling out Jake Perrick's gun and snapping a warning shot at the three riders bearing in from the north. They were still some distance away, all firing freely. He looked for Melissa, to be certain she was close by. She was not at his side and he slowed his stride.

He saw her then, a small shape lying near the wagon.

"Melissa!" he yelled.

He glanced at the approaching riders to see how near they were. He took careful aim at the nearest man and threw a shot at him. He saw the horse veer away and heard the rider shout an oath. It was Jake Perrick. He was using a rifle and he fired it now with one hand. Santell heard the bullet thunk into the ground only a yard away. He snapped another bullet at the man and then, wheeling, he ran to Melissa. Stooping swiftly he gathered her into his arms. She was unconscious, knocked out by the leap from the hurtling wagon. Waiting no longer Santell started for the brush at a plunging, rocking gait.

There was not a moment to be lost. He had not hit any of the three riders; he had merely turned them aside. They would all be driving down upon them again. Bullets were already thudding into the ground about his feet and whispering by his head as he ran. He was doing his best, hindered by Melissa's weight. Perrick was playing for keeps now. He no longer meant only to halt them, he meant to kill. Only the darkness and their own galloping horses were making it a difficult task.

It seemed the brush receded before him with each lunging step he took. But finally they reached it. He did not slow down but hurried on, turning sharp left as soon as they were well within the shadows. Melissa's weight, small as it was, hindered him and he was tiring fast. But he could not pause. He had to get as far as possible before he halted.

He heard Perrick yell and somewhere back along the fringe there came an answer. They were stalled there, at least for a few minutes while they sought to learn in which direction he had turned. He might have swung left or right. Or even gone straight on, boring deeper into the brush. They would probably split up now, each man taking a different way. But they would proceed cautiously. They were respecting his gun. He cut deeper then, going to his right, striking toward the mountain where the brush would be in thicker stands and there would be a better chance for locating a good hiding place.

Melissa began to struggle in his arms and he dropped his glance to her. The pale oval of her face was upturned to him. She looked, in the meager light, as if she were sleeping, her eyes closed, her features soft and calm. Her lips were slightly parted, full and smooth — as Eva's had been. He lifted his gaze quickly to the indistinct trail winding ahead, not liking the thought. She stirred again.

"Put me down!"

Her voice was low, surprising him with its insistence. He was moving along at a fairly fast pace, making good use of the moments alloted them. Without looking down at her he said, "We've got no time to lose. You sure you can walk?"

"I can walk," she declared stubbornly.

He halted and let her feet drop to the ground, maintaining his support of her shoulders by keeping his arm around her. She came upright, staggering a little as she tried to regain balance. For a moment she clung tightly to him. Off in the north a ragged flash of lightning broke the dark sky, followed at once by a peal of thunder.

Almost brusquely he said, "We can't rest here. Maybe I'd better carry you for a time yet. You got a bad rap on the head when you jumped."

"I'm all right," she murmured. "Just let me take your hand."

He felt her fingers lace into his own and they moved on. She came close behind him, stumbling a bit to keep up with his long steps. But she made no sound, uttered no protest at his breathless pace. She stayed with him and when they finally gained the first ledge of rock and he halted, she sank to the ground, going into a small heap. She was near exhaustion.

His manner toward her changed swiftly. "I'm sorry," he said, dropping to his knee beside her. "But it couldn't be helped. We had to get away fast."

She nodded. "Can we — do we stay here?" she gasped.

"We can but we ought to move on. After you've had a little rest. It would be risky, staying this close. The farther away we are come daylight, the better."

At once she struggled to her feet. "I'm ready," she said.

He grinned at her in the darkness. "Not yet. We can spare another minute or two."

"I won't hold you back," she said in a firm voice. "I won't be the cause of them catching you. Now that the horses are lost, you'll have to go on without me. I'll find a place to hide. I'll manage somehow."

He took her by the shoulders, moved by her small determination. "I'll hear no more of that," he said shaking her gently. "We're in this thing together now, whether we like it or not. What happens from now on happens to both of us."

She settled back down and he stood for a moment listening into the darkness. A storm was rolling in. The sky was almost entirely sealed over now and the break of lightning and hammer of thunder were becoming more frequent. He could now scarcely make out Melissa's features although she was so close he could feel the warm, sweetness of her breath against his cheek, hear the drawing of it through her parted lips. The long hunger of the man surged through him and he had a sudden urge to reach out and draw her to him, crush his mouth against hers. But it passed as quickly. The powerful, restricting memory of Eva crowded in between them, getting in his way, placing its bitter warning upon him. In the charcoal depths of the forest, a rancorous mood swept over him, possessing his body, his mind, turning down the corners of his lips and narrowing his eyes.

In a sharp voice he said, "Let's move on."

She stepped away from him. "I'm ready."

She reached for his hand and they started again. Santell, disturbed by his own thoughts, kept close to the rocks, saying nothing. They moved quietly, avoiding the swishing brush, going well around anything, any dense thickets that might betray their presence. There was no telling where Perrick and the others were; they could be far off to the northward, or they could be only a few steps away.

A gash of lightning ripped open the ebony sky, an accompaniment of thunder riding close. The storm was coming fast. There was hope in that, Santell decided; rain would destroy any trail Charley Ironhead might otherwise be able to follow. But it would make the going bad for them.

They reached a short bluff and came to a stop. Santell was undecided whether to swing back and climb upon it or stay along its foot. On top, he reasoned, they might be safer. They would be above the level of the forest's floor and thus be in a position to observe the posse's activities. But in so doing they would be isolating themselves, leaving but one escape route up the steep side of the mountain. And they would sacrifice time in mounting to the crest of the ledge, time that might better be spent in pushing on southward through the brush. Better to stay on the level ground and keep —

"Over here, Marshal!"

Jake Perrick's strident voice, startlingly close, shattered Santell's thoughts.

His fingers tightened about Melissa's. Making no sound whatever, he drew her deeper into the shadows beneath the bluff.

105

They were going nowhere — at least, not for some time.

Shotgun Travers, several hours ahead of Santell and Melissa York, lay in the protective shadows of a thick greasewood clump and waited for nightfall. His horse grazed in a low hollow some twenty yards away, well below the average level of the plains, unable to be seen by anyone scouting the country.

Now was the time for care, he knew. A man crossing the flat land was visible for miles. It had not been difficult to escape Harry Decket back in the hills. After his initial bolt from the clutches of the would-be marshal, he had merely ducked into the thick forest growth and from a distance of only a few hundred yards, observed with satisfaction Decket's rage and eventual departure for Sutterville. He had trailed the little man at safe distance for a mile or so, assuring himself the lawman was going on to the settlement and not just working a ruse by which he hoped to draw him out. But Decket had pressed on and Travers had turned back, swinging south in a wide circle.

He had lied to Decket, of course, about his familiarity with the country. He knew it like the back of his hand and long before the marshal was riding off to Sutterville an escape plan had been shaping up in his mind. He would push southward, bearing always east until he reached the outflung edge of the hills. There he would remain until dark, after which he would start across the flats, moving only at night, doing his resting and sleeping in any of the numberless ravines and swales during the daylight hours.

He would head for Luceroville, a Mexican village lying about halfway across the New Mexico plateau on the road to Texas. There, slipping in unseen, he could hole up for a few days with Procopio Gonzales, an old friend with whom he used to ride. He could rely on old Copio; he would be safe there at least for a week or so, and by that time Harry Decket would have either given up the chase or else be far off in some different area looking for him.

It would be easy. All he had to do was reach the village unseen, either by Decket and the posse or any of the few inhabitants of Luceroville. And that should be easy. Of course, he was beginning to feel the drag of hunger and the need for water. But he could stand it; it wouldn't be the first time he had gone without food and drink. Anyway, a man could endure anything knowing that escape from Harry Decket depended upon it.

He glanced skyward. It looked like rain. That would solve his thirst.

9

The tree tops had begun to weave gently with the rushing of the storm. In the stillness Jake Perrick had seemed no more than steps away. In reality he was much farther. Peering through the screen of brush Clay Santell could make out his heavy, gross outline along with those of the two other men standing near their horses in a small clearing.

A match flared and a cigarette was lit. Tex London's voice drawled, "You going to tell the marshal about Travers beltin' you one and getting away, Jake?" There was a lazy insolence in the man's tone.

After a long pause Perrick answered. "Well, now, I don't see no cause for telling him anything like that. Let's just say we spotted them, him and the gal high-tailin' for these here trees. It being dark as the inside of a rabbit hole, they just naturally give us the slip."

There was no immediate response from the two men. Perrick's voice, suddenly sharp and querulous, demanded, "We all agreed on that being the way of it?"

"All right with me, Jake," Tex London murmured.

"How about you, Cunningham?"

"You're doin' the talkin'. I reckon that'll be the way it will be said."

"Good," Perrick said with a deep sigh. "No use us telling that little squirt anything we don't have to." He stopped, adding after a moment, "There they come now. The marshal's going to be real disappointed when he don't find his man Travers just layin' out there cold dead on the ground for him."

Harry Decket and the Indian rode into the clearing. The marshal said nothing but sat quietly in his saddle, apparently studying the men before him. Charley Ironhead dismounted and joined the circle made by Perrick and the others.

"Well, where is he?" Decket demanded finally in sharp-edged impatience.

"He got away, Marshal," Perrick replied with an ambiguous wave of his hand. "We jumped him back there on the flats but he beat us to the trees. Then we lost him."

A low, savage oath ripped from Decket's lips. "Dammit all! Can't nobody do anything right? Might have known you'd mess it up." He raged on for a minute, smashing his doubled fist into his open palm. "Any ideas where he went?"

"South, right straight ahead of you. Know that to be a fact 'cause we spread out and had a look. He sure didn't double back up or we'd have run into him."

"How about that mountain there? He's no cripple. Why couldn't he had started climbing that just as easy —"

"Side of that hill is nothin' but loose rock. A man would sound like a troop of blue-belly cavalry trying to move up there. Nope, he sure went south."

Again Harry Decket was silent. It was too dark for Santell to see his face other than its vague outline, but he was recalling its cruel lines, the small, sharp eyes. The mouth would be a hard slash, bitter and unrelenting.

"Well, what's the next move? You got any plan or do we just squat here on our hind ends until daylight and then put the Indian on his trail?"

"No use waiting," Perrick said unhurriedly. "Rain's probably going to spoil any trackin' for Charley anyway. I figured we'd spread out across this grove, about ten, twelve feet apart, and start walkin'. That'll flush them out."

"Them?" Decket's question was like a quick, small explosion in the night. "Who's with him?"

"A gal. He joined up with her back there on the mountain. They was in her wagon when we spotted them. Wagon hit a wash and flopped over, dumpin' them out."

"A girl," Decket said with slow satisfaction. "That's fine, fine. It will slow him down considerable."

In the tense, breathless moments, deep in the brush, Santell felt Melissa stir beside him, Decket's words having their strong effect upon her. He tightened his fingers upon her small hand reassuringly.

Decket came off his saddle. "Going to be hard to do anything without a light. Let the Indian follow along with the horses. Four of us can work this grove. It's not wide."

Santell watched the dim shapes of the others move to Charley Ironhead and hand over their mounts. The moment was turning critical. In a short time they would form a cordon and move toward Melissa and himself. Even in the dark they stood little chance of escape. They would be caught in front of the moving men unable to turn in any direction.

Santell's hand dropped to the gun at his hip. And slid away. There was no answer there, not with Melissa in his care. Alone he would have chosen this moment to make his stand, banking on shooting his way through their line and capturing a horse. But that was out. He raked his mind for an idea, any idea that would offer them a chance for escape. As it was, they were pinned down tight. They could not move, yet it was suicide to remain. It might come to a showdown after all. It could be that was the only answer. His hand dropped to Perrick's pistol at his side. He drew it out and noiselessly flipped open the loading gate. He had not taken time to reload it. There were five empty shells in the cylinder and he punched them out. He slipped a cartridge from his belt and pushed it against one of the openings. It would not fit. Disappointment slogged through him. He picked up one of the empty brass cases and held it between his thumb and forefinger in the blackness, matching it against one of the cartridges from his belt. They were different sizes. Perrick's gun was of a smaller calibre.

A surge of frustrated anger swept through him. Why couldn't he have one piece of luck? But he made no sound, only replacing the empty, useless pistol in his holster and dropping the shells to the ground.

He remembered then Perrick's remarks concerning the mountain, the loose shale and the noise anyone moving on the slope would create. At once his hopes lifted; it was a long chance but at least, it was a chance. He laid his finger against Melissa's lips, warning her to silence. Dropping to his knees he crawled out of the thicket, searching the soft earth as he did so for a stone. He found one, about the size of a balled fist and paused. The Indian now had all the ponies under his control. Decket and the rest of the posse were beginning to spread out, forming their line.

Moving a step further away from the thicket to be certain he would not strike any brush he hurled the rock over the posse's heads, up onto the side of the mountain. It struck with a loud clatter, dislodging a hatfull of smaller stones that rattled noisily downward. It was an ancient ruse but it worked.

"Hey! Back there! There he goes!" Perrick yelled.

"He's not below us, he's above us," Decket said in heavy disgust, "Come on, get over there after him before he gives us the slip again."

The marshal wheeled about and broke into a run, heading away from Santell and Melissa still crouching in the blackness. They waited until the others, including Charley Ironhead, had swung about and were crashing off after Decket and then they moved away from the bluff.

"Hurry," Santell whispered.

A roll of thunder came again, much closer this time. Santell felt a drop of rain upon his wrist as they slipped off, silent as moonlight, into the darkness. They kept low, stooping beneath the crown of brush. Back of them the sounds of the search were plain; the slashing about, the flat clatter of rocks displaced and shifting on the slope, the muffled curses and impatient shouts.

The single drop of rain increased to a mild sprinkle and soon to a steady shower, cool and soaking. Santell did not stop to seek shelter but pressed on with Melissa at his heels.

"Rain will save our necks," he said after they had covered a good distance. "That Indian can't trail us now. But we still got to get as far away from here as we can before they wake up to the fact that it wasn't us back there on the mountain. Can't risk their just stumbling across us after all this hard work."

Their passage began to slow, however, as the country grew steadily rougher. To counteract this, Santell began to swing eastward, away from the mountain slope, pointing at a long tangent for the plains. They could move much faster, he thought, where the brush was more sparse and there were no rocks impeding the trail. The rain was a hindrance now, having graduated from a shower to a full-scale storm that lashed at them viciously. Lightning flashed with clocklike regularity and the grove was in a constant din of thunder. They were wet to the skin and bitterly cold.

"I'm freezing!" Melissa chattered when they stopped for breath. Santell had chosen a thick, closely spread cedar tree that gave them a fair amount of protection.

He drew her close to him, pressing his body to hers, trying to impart some warmth. "How far to that old way station you were telling me about?"

"Another ten or twelve miles, I'm not sure. I don't know just where we are."

"Place sounds like our best bet. We'll try and make it there and hide out for a spell."

"Won't Jake think of that, too?"

"Likely. But don't think he'll head there tonight. They probably figure we're back there somewhere in the trees or in a cave maybe on the mountainside. My guess is they'll think they've got us trapped along there and they'll find a dry place to wait out daylight."

"Wish we could find a cave. Any place out

of this rain. I was never so tired. Or wet and cold."

He tried to comfort her, awkwardly patting her shoulder. "It's a tough spot for you, I know. But we got to try and make that way station. Think you can hold out that far?"

"I'll try," she replied.

They moved out from beneath the cedar's meager protection into the driving storm. The rain had swept down from the high peaks and it was striking now at their backs with stinging force. Santell guided Melissa to a position a half-step in front of him, using his own body as a shield for hers. They walked blindly, periodically wading through ankle-deep pools, pushing through brush that flayed them like sopping whips, wetting them all the more if such was possible.

They reached the edge of the trees and stopped. The plains, dark and wide, rolled out before them, the rain looking like a silver, waving curtain in the lightning's lurid flashes.

"That way station — south from here?" Santell asked, letting his gaze follow along the dark edge of trees.

Melissa said, "Yes. Keep along the mountain."

They started again, staying within the

trees, which offered some protection from the storm. But it mattered little; both were drenched. Santell felt as if he were walking through knee-deep water, his boots were so full. And now, to worsen matters, the wind had begun to rise, sharp-edged and hard-driven.

Melissa was tiring fast. The long hike, the load of her dripping clothing, the clutching, hindering brush, all had taken their terrific toll of her strength. Santell paused more often, giving her more frequent rests. He had offered to carry her if need be but she steadfastly refused to burden him with her weight. And as the minutes passed he began to realize they had small chance of reaching the shelter of the abandoned stage stop. He began to look around for some suitable spot where they could wait out the night, any place out of the blast of wind and rain. To hope it would be dry was asking too much.

Utilizing the vivid flashes of lightning, he kept his glance probing their surroundings. They were in a sparse grove now where even the brush was low and scattered. It became clearer to him with each step that they would have to cut back toward the mountain if they were to locate a halfway acceptable haven. He did not like that; such would take them toward Harry Decket and his posse. It would be a little like helping that man in his relentless search.

But if Decket and his men had settled down for the remainder of the night, they would lose little. He was fairly certain they had done just that. They could have accomplished little, thrashing about in the storm, and since they had the vast advantage of being mounted while their quarry struggled along on foot, Decket would feel pretty sure of all things. The slim little lawman, however, was a hard one to figure. He was a grim, ceaseless pursuer, one that would allow few things to deter him and then for only a brief time.

Santell halted again, standing hard by a thick and wildly swaying pine. He drew Melissa against him as he had been doing the past hour, draping his arms over her slim shoulders to ward off the wind and rain and give her what warmth he could. Lightning ripped across the black sky, flooding the plains and forest alike with its bluish, eerie glow. Santell's heart skipped a beat!

Not fifty yards ahead he had caught a fragmentary glimpse of horses! At least, he thought it was horses he had seen, standing with heads down in the pouring rain. He said nothing to Melissa but remained still, his eyes fastened to that point where he had seen, or imagined he had seen, the animals. He awaited breathlessly the next illuminating flash.

The flood of light came again, vivid and brief. It was horses! Two of them — a team still in harness. Melissa's team, of course, he realized. When the wagon had overturned they had broken free and run until tired.

He still said nothing to Melissa but started forward, proceeding slowly and cautiously, keeping within the dark cover of trees. The last thing he wanted to do now was startle the ponies, start them running madly off through the night again. Not only could they get Melissa and himself to the shelter of the way station but they would afford a means for crossing the plains to Splendor, to Hall McGivern and immunity forever from Harry Decket. And home for Melissa York.

When he judged they had reached a point just opposite where the horses were standing, he again halted. He told Melissa then about their good luck, cautioning her to remain quiet while he captured the animals. He worked his way to the extreme edge of the brush and waited for the next explosion of lightning. It came. He saw he was just below the team. He stalled out the next break of light and when it was spent, hurried through the blackness to the horses. They did not bolt at his approach but stood fast, seemingly glad for human presence on such a fearful night. He took a firm grip on the headstall of one and then called out to Melissa.

Together they pulled off the harness, leaving only the bridles. Mounting was a chore, the horses' hides being wet and slick and their own clothing sopping wet. But they eventually accomplished it and headed out south. The way station was not such a distant hope now.

10

Riding the horses bareback, and wet as they were, they pushed on. Traveling was less arduous but no more comfortable. The wind was cold, knifing through the storm that was passing now on to the dark prairie. The arroyos were beginning to flow, shouldering their surging loads of roily, silted water down from the mountain peaks and crevasses. Several times they had to stop and check the power and depth of some foaming current before continuing.

It was well after midnight when the squat, rambling shape of the way station loomed up in the darkness. They stopped behind the outlying, crumbling stables and Santell, not underestimating Harry Decket for a moment, went on foot to investigate. The huge, single room of the abandoned structure was empty, as was the barn. He returned to Melissa much relieved.

They put the horses in the stable, finding a small amount of old hay in one corner of a stall. Then they made their way to the main building. The rain had all but stopped. The wind, however, offset that relief by settling down to a wild, stiff bluster that bit deeply and cut like a muleskinner's whip, magnifying their chill. They hurried into the doorless station, grateful to be out of the blow.

It was pitch black. Leaving Melissa in one corner out of the wind's reach, Santell prowled the room. He located a lantern but discovered at once it contained no oil and was therefore useless. Near it he found a stub of candle. Most of his matches were wet but one finally caught flame and he set the candle to going.

It was a square room, rough-beamed and low-ceilinged. All of the windows were without glass and had been curtained with gunny sacks, which flapped and bulged now in the gale. There was no door. Sand had drifted in through the opening and lay in a thick, conical dune on the threshold. Against one wall straw had been matted to form a bed and upon this lay a ragged, gray woolen blanket. The fireplace was a large rock oblong, half-filled with powdery ashes that lifted and fell restlessly as each succeeding gust of wind swirled down the chimney or lashed across the floor.

Santell placed the candle on the mantle, throwing a yellow light upon a faded picture of a stagecoach rounding a mountain turn while a small party of feathered Indians looked on from their spotted ponies. He studied the cheap print for a moment and then said, "I'll locate some wood for a fire. You better shed those wet clothes. Use that old blanket. It's dusty but dry."

Melissa glanced at the tattered rag. "I can dry out in front of the fire."

"Suit yourself," Santell replied, too weary to argue the question. He walked outside into the wild night.

He located some lengths of lumber, dry and rotting, in the barn. Gathering up a full arm's load, he returned to the station. Melissa was standing in the corner where he had left her, the blanket drawn about her. A puddle of water lay on the floor where she had wrung out her shirt and levis which now hung from the mantle. Santell made no comment but he was glad she had accepted his advice. Now was no time for modesty; a few hours more in those sopping, wet clothes could mean pneumonia, a severe cold at best. For himself he was less concerned. The bitter winter on the Colorado slopes had toughened him to such things and conditions like this were little more than discomforts.

With a handful of the dry straw he got a fire going and within a few minutes the corner where they stood began to fill with a cheery warmth despite the wind's thrusting through the doorway and tearing at the makeshift curtains on the windows. Standing there before the flames, soaking up the heat, Santell watched the color creep slowly back into Melissa's cheeks. She had found a pin somewhere and had fastened the blanket above her breasts, leaving only her neck and head visible. Her black hair was down about her shoulders and she was leaning forward fluffing it, drying it before the fire. It shimmered as the flames played against its dark sheen.

Santell's throat tightened. There was a hunger burning steadily within him. He struggled with his own thoughts, trying to segregate them, organize them and come to some understanding with himself about this

Melissa York. He had known her now little more than a half-dozen hours. Yet it seemed timeless. It came to him then that he would miss her when this trouble was over and all things were finished and she was gone. And then Santell frowned, angrily stirred by that thought. Why should he miss her? She meant nothing to him — no woman ever again would! She was just so much excess weight, a measure of trouble added to his own that he could not avoid and, in all human decency, could not help assuming. He should be glad when she was off his hands and safe in a new home of her own.

Melissa straightened up from her task of hair drying and reversed the shirt and pants hanging from the mantle. A continuous drip of water fell from their lowest points, creating another puddle. But they were drying. Santell looked at her, softening a little. She was so very small, so slender. He wondered how she had been able to stand that long, terrible flight through the forest.

He said then, "How about your — your other things? They ought to dry, too."

Without looking at him she replied, "They're all right. I wrung them out and put them back on."

Santell nodded. He was beginning to feel the weight of the hours. He had been tired after the long ride across the mountains, and to that had been added the events of the evening and the subsequent escape through the storm. Moving to the pile of straw he began to scuff it into separate piles. Melissa watched him with expressionless eyes.

"You best keep that blanket," he said, coming finally back to the fire. He squatted down and tossed more wood onto the flames.

"I'll wait until my clothes are dry and put them back on. Warmer that way."

Santell murmured, "Sure." He was aware of her sudden withdrawal from him, of almost a fear that was in her eyes. He wanted to reassure her, tell her no harm would come to her. But somehow he could not find the words. Outside, beyond the thick adobe brick walls, the wind tore at the building with lifting force, rattling loose boards, whistling and moaning around the corners like souls lost in a labyrinth of hell. The coldness was sharp, felt only a few feet away from the fire's reach.

"Reckon we better keep this fire going all night," he said. "I better rustle more wood."

"Don't go!" she cried, unexpectedly. There was a high note of fear in her voice.

He turned to her in mild surprise. He had

not realized she was frightened. She had a woman's feelings after all. He had thought her almost emotionless, more like a man where fear and hardship were concerned. But she did react as he would expect her to under trying conditions. He said, "Don't worry. I'll only go to the barn. Just take a minute."

"I know, Clay," she said, keeping her face turned from him. "But don't go. Please. I'm afraid. I don't know what it is, but I'm afraid."

He studied her taut face for a moment. Then, "All right, Melissa. Maybe we have enough, anyway."

He started to say more, paused, caught up sharply by a new and different sound, audible beneath the howl of the wind. It sounded much like the drag of a boot heel upon gravel. He spun to the doorway, hand dropping to the useless gun at his hip. He could bluff but no more than that. The shadowy outlines of three men stood suddenly just within. A small cry wrenched from Melissa's lips as she stepped close to him. Santell's first thought was of Harry Decket, that the marshal had not, after all, given up until daylight but had pressed on ignoring the storm, guessing they would seek the shelter of the way station.

But he saw then it was not Decket nor any member of the posse. Three strangers, all hard-faced, gaunt men who looked as if they had come far and fast and who could not stop for long. All were heavily armed. One of them, a thick-set, bow-legged individual who had drawn his gun, brushed his hat to the back of his head and advanced a step. His lips were cracked into a whisker-shrouded leer.

"What do you know about this! A cowboy and his lady friend! You all got it mighty nice here, folks."

Santell met his insolent, inferential stare with level eyes. "We're dry, if that's what you mean," he said in a winter-cold voice. "What do you want?"

"Why, just to get in out of the weather, that's all."

The other pair drifted closer to the fireplace. They had traveled through the rain also, their faded, worn clothing still plastered wetly to their bodies. They were younger than the first man who seemed to be the leader. They said nothing, merely watched with hard, glittering eyes and listened well. Outlaws on the run, Santell guessed.

"Keep moving," he said then in a tough voice. He knew their kind. He had been up against dozens of them and the best defense was always offense. "No room in this place for all of us. Use the barn."

The whiskered leader laughed. "Now, you wouldn't turn us out on a night like this," he chided, wagging his gun for emphasis. He was looking beyond Santell to Melissa standing slightly behind the big man. His eyes flickered to the clothing hanging against the mantle and came back at once to her blanketed figure. "We sure don't aim to cause you no harm, mister."

Santell repeated it. "Use the barn! We're in here first."

The outlaw's face settled into bleak angles. "This suits us, don't it, boys?"

One of the younger men nodded. He slanted a glance at Santell. "We won't give you trouble. We just need a dry place to catch a little sleep."

Santell considered for a long minute. The odds were all against him anyway, he couldn't press his luck too far. Best to play along, play it straight. He said, grudgingly, "All right. But keep your place. Stay on that side of the fireplace. This side belongs to me."

" 'Course," the outlaw leader rumbled. He slid his well worn pistol into its holster and extended his hairy hands, palms foremost, to the flames. "Real fierce storm out there tonight."

"Bad enough," Santell replied.

"Reckon you'd better trot out and get more wood. You ain't got enough to last the night."

Santell favored the man with a scornful look. "You want more wood, you get it," he said and swung back to the straw pallets he was preparing.

Melissa moved to the fireplace, reclaiming her steaming garments. Santell heard her gasp suddenly and spun about. The outlaw had seized her by the wrist and was trying to draw her to him.

"How about bein' my lady friend for the rest of the night, girlie?"

Santell took one long, lunging stride. He drove his knotted fist into the man's smirking face, knocking him backwards and into the far wall. Gun out, he snarled, "One more stunt like that and I'll kill you! Nobody lays a hand on my wife!"

The outlaw stared up at him. His hand, poised above the butt of his pistol, drifted slowly away. In the tense, violence-laden moments there were no sounds save the wind and the soft crackling of the fire.

"Either stay on your side of that fireplace or get out!" Santell's face was a mask of suppressed fury. "Make your choice!"

One of the younger outlaws spoke up. "All right, mister. Just you calm down. We don't want no trouble. Grover'll leave your woman alone. Reckon he didn't know she was your wife."

"You're right he'll leave her alone or you got yourself a dead partner to tote out of here!"

Santell pivoted to Melissa. "Get to bed."

She looked at him with wide eyes, not sure of his meaning, disturbed by his tone. And she was uncertain of his intentions, still mistrusting him as a man. He dropped to the pallet and, gun still in hand, threw a glance across the room. The outlaw had got back to his feet and was again with his friends before the fire. Melissa, pulling free her levis and shirt, came to where Santell waited. In a low voice he said, "Forget those clothes. Lay down. This is no time to be trying to dress."

Melissa opened her mouth to protest. She could pull the clothing on under the blanket. That way there would be nothing for them to see except her camouflaged movements.

"Do what I tell you!" Santell gritted in a low whisper. His voice was savage with its insistence. He knew well what the fired-up

130

imagination of a man such as Grover was capable of. And they were three to his one, all armed. He'd have no chance to protect her if they rushed him. "Do it unless you want to spend the night with Grover there."

Obediently she lay down. Santell pulled the straw up around her, draping the near-dry clothing over her feet.

Grover watched with covert eyes. Santell, finished with his arrangements, leaned back against the rough wall, his attention riveted to the three men.

"Don't forget this," he said in a cool, calm voice. "First man to step this side of that fireplace gets a bullet through his guts. My wife needs some rest. I aim to see she gets it."

"Didn't know she was your wife," Grover mumbled through his crushed lips. "I ain't touchin' no man's wife."

"You know it now," Santell snapped. "Just don't let it slip your mind."

The other two outlaws had settled down before the flickering flames, one stretching out full length on the floor, the other sitting hunched foward, resting on his updrawn knees. Grover tossed more wood on the fire and began to turn his body before the heat, systematically warming and drying all sides like a chicken being roasted on a spit. The temperature of the room increased and Santell found himself fighting to keep awake.

He dropped his gaze to Melissa. She was sound asleep, completely exhausted, unable to hold out longer against the push of fatigue. Her face, the only part visible in the blanket, was serene and childlike. He noticed how long her dark lashes were, how they lay snug against the creamy tan of her cheeks. Her brows were black, too, and thick for those of a woman. Her lips were faintly parted and again Santell had that unwelcome feeling of kinship, of closeness to her and that promise of loss when they would part. Feeling Grover's hard and completely suspicious gaze upon him in that moment, he bent forward and kissed her lightly, full on the lips. She stirred and came awake instantly, anger moving swiftly across her features.

"Don't!" she said in a low, tense voice. "I should have known! You're no better than Jake Perrick or any other man."

Santell crushed his mouth against hers, shutting off the hurried flow of wrathful words, choking them back to prevent their being heard. "Hush," he muttered, "we're being watched. I'm not enjoying this any more than you but if you want to leave here alive, act like a wife!"

Melissa relaxed under his tight grasp. Some of the bright fury left her eyes but the mistrust, or a measure of it, yet remained there. Santell straightened up. Grover was still watching, his face a dark study.

He said, "Reckon I'd kill a man, too, for a woman like your wife, was she mine."

Santell made no reply, merely holding his gaze.

"Don't reckon I'll even ever get the chance," the outlaw continued. "Don't ever see her kind around the places where I go. You best stay wide awake, mister. I might just forget a few things."

"I'll be awake," Santell promised softly.

Grover turned his attention to the fire. After a moment he lay down, shoulders touching those of his fellow rider, his brooding hard-lined face toward the flames. Santell waited, seeing the man's body gradually slacken as sleep overtook him. The man, prone on the floor, snored gently.

He struggled to keep his eyes open, to keep alert and ready for trouble. Melissa was sleeping again, a small frown wedged between her closed eyes. The fire had begun to dwindle but he would not replenish it. Let Grover or one of his companions do that. They were closer and anyway, he would take no chances of placing himself within their reach. He glanced toward the doorway. It seemed to be growing lighter.

Sunrise was not far off.

11

The cold, drilling deeply into his bones, brought Santell awake. He glanced first to Melissa. She was still asleep, breathing with soft regularity, resting entirely. He looked then to the fire; it had faded to glowing coals. And the outlaws were gone.

He got quickly to his feet, a vague alarm lifting within him. Tossing a handful of straw on the ashes he blew it into flame, adding the last of the wood when it caught. Melissa stirred and sat up.

He wheeled to face her and she saw the strong worry in his eyes. "What's the matter?"

Santell shook his head. "I don't know. But there's something. I fell asleep and sometime after that our friends left. They wouldn't have gone so quiet if they hadn't had something in mind." He stiffened. "The horses!"

He spun about and ran through the doorway. The wind had slackened little and it struck at him now, viciously, when he came into the open yard, buffeting him soundly as he ran in long-legged steps for the stable. Entering, he looked hurriedly about. A sigh moved through his lips. The dim outlines of two horses standing in the gloomy depths of the barn had answered his question.

And then a frown crossed his face. One of the animals had turned to look at him. It had a white blaze across its long nose; neither of Melissa's ponies had such a marking. A curse slipped from Santell's mouth. Neither of the horses were Melissa's. They were strangers, well worn and badly spent, of little use to anyone. The outlaws had simply exchanged two of their ridden-out mounts for a pair of almost fresh animals. It had been done in a rush, Santell saw. They had not taken time to switch bridles.

Santell, a mixture of anger and disappointment threading through him, went back to the way station. The loss of the team was a serious blow; with it they were assured of a means for keeping beyond Decket's reaching fingers long enough to reach Splendor. With that pair of wind-broken bonebags they now had, there was small chance. But they had no other choice.

The sun was a transparent, blackly edged silver disc in the east, almost obscured by the slate overcast. The rain was over, having spent itself somewhere in the rolling dis-

135

tances of the prairie, and now the wind was having its free way. It scoured the hills and flats, already starting to wring the new moisture from the soil. In another two hours there would be sand flying fine and sharp across the mesas.

Santell reached the building and turned in. Melissa, fully dressed now, stood before the blazing fire. Trying to withhold the desperateness of their situation from her, he said, "We got horse-traded by our friends."

"Horse-traded?"

"They took ours — yours. Left us a couple of nags in their place. Afraid they're not much."

She stared at him for a moment and then dipped her head, trying to hide from him, as he was from her, the hopelessness she felt. "Don't worry too much about it," she murmured after a time. "At least we've got horses. That's more than we had for a time last night. Even they give us a chance to get through."

"Not a good one," he said tiredly. "They can't stand much and we can't push them hard. But if they'll just hold out at a walk and Decket doesn't crowd us too hard, we might get through."

"Then we better start now and waste no more time," she said, gathering up the old blanket. "I'll take this along. We may need it again."

She paused, meeting his eyes squarely. "About last night, Clay. I'm sorry about it — about the way I acted. I guess I just didn't understand at first. I thought —"

"Never mind," he said gruffly. "I had to play it that way for your sake as well as mine. I know you've got mighty small use for any man and you likely have your own good reasons for feeling that way. No matter, it's your business. And that's as it should be. You look after yours and I'll look after mine."

For a moment she made no reply, her eyes spreading a bit at his harsh rebuff. Finally, in a low voice she said, "I think I understand," and moved for the doorway.

Santell followed her out into the shrieking wind and together they walked to the barn. There was one thing in their favor, he noticed as they crossed the narrow yard: the blow, like the rain, was from the mountains. It would be against their backs.

The horses were even worse than he had at first feared. They were so near exhaustion it was necessary to haze them from the barn. They walked slowly, heads down, and Santell could barely hope for just one hour's use of them before they collapsed.

Looking them over in the gray light, he said, "What they need is rest. A day, at least. And plenty to eat."

"They don't look as if they could get far," Melissa admitted.

"If we could stay holed up here until dark," Santell mused, half-aloud, "the rest would do us all some good."

He swung about, looking toward the north. For a moment he remained poised there, his eyes sharp under his wide-brimmed hat, the strong, hard angle of his jaw showing faintly white beneath its carpet of black whiskers. Abruptly he wheeled about. "We can forget that," he stated flatly.

"What is it?" Melissa asked.

"A rider," he answered, pointing. "Just coming up on the skyline, near the trees."

She followed his leveled arm. "I see him," she said after a time. "Look, there's another!"

"Three more, coming out of the brush," Santell added. Five horsemen etched against the gray sky. "That's Decket and his posse. They're headed this way, coming to have their look for us at this place."

"We better not wait any longer."

Santell nodded. He shuttled his gaze over the landscape, hazy now in the grip of the wind. The prairie dipped into a shallow

138

swale a short distance below them, to their right. If they could remain unseen until they gained that depression, they would immediately drop below the level of the horizon and could proceed without being seen by the posse.

He outlined the plan to Melissa. "We'll move so that the building will stand between us and them until we reach the hollow."

She nodded her understanding. "The horses?"

"Lead them. Let them walk at least until we get tired. That will save them some. Then maybe they can carry us for a spell."

Again Melissa indicated her understanding with a slight motion of her head. She took up the reins of one horse and started off, getting first behind the way station's bulk. Santell threw another calculating glance toward Decket and his men and started after her, his horse plodding tiredly at his heels. It would be easy to keep the old structure between them until they reached the cover of the swale; he was more worried about their tracks. The wind would not have wiped them entirely away by the time the riders reached the yard and even if he took the necessary minutes to erase them himself, Charley Ironhead would quickly find the signs he needed to piece together the story. Santell shrugged. He was getting jumpy; no use being disturbed over that; there wasn't anything he could do about it.

They soon reached the swale and turned back eastward. The wind maintained its pressure, beginning to sting now with its particles of fine sand snatched up from the drying earth. Overhead a lead-gray sky held firm, an over-arching bowl up which the sun climbed slowly, barely discernible through the mounting pall.

Santell began to feel hunger and realized Melissa must be in similar straits. Otherwise, he did not feel so bad. His shoulder had lost its stiffness sometime during the night and the wound left by Harry Decket's rifle bullet was little more than an irritation. But he was tired clear through. It seemed like weeks since he had slept. The two or three hours stolen during the previous night had done him little good. But there was no rest for them now. They moved on, daring not to slow down with Decket again closing in. They followed out the depression and when they came to its end and once again stood upon a level with the surrounding land, they halted.

Santell swung his search to the west, to where the way station lay. Five riders were indistinctly outlined against the backdrop of mountains. Charley Ironhead had not taken long to find the trail.

"They're coming," he said, laying his fingers on Melissa's wrist to draw her attention. "We'll ride now. We've got to move faster."

She said nothing but turned to her horse and pulled herself upon its back. Santell followed and they struck out. It was a relief to get off his feet but they were moving little faster than they had been on foot.

The wind's velocity increased, laden now with sand that stung and filled their eyes and mouths. Melissa pulled the blanket salvaged from the way station from beneath her and tried to wrap it around her body for protection. A fierce gust snatched it up, wrenched it from her and hurled it away. It was gone in an instant, a dark, irregular ball tumbling across the flats.

Santell guided his horse in close to her. He had pulled his hat down low and drawn his shirt collar, upturned and buttoned, over his mouth. Only his nose and eyes were visible. He drew her notice to this ancient cowboy's trick and at once she followed his suggestion with her own collar.

The wind was not so cold. That helped considerably. But it maintained its bruising force and the sand was an ever-present enemy, biting at their hands and faces and other exposed parts of their bodies, harassing and blinding the worn horses. Yet it had become a welcome cover. Visibility had closed down upon them; they could see no more than a hundred yards and as time wore on that shortened to such a degree that soon their world was limited to fifty feet or less. It was like being in a swirling, choking prison but it had its one advantage. Decket nor his men could no longer see them.

Shortly after noon Santell's horse began to limp. He dismounted and made a brief examination of the hoof. He found nothing wrong and this meant one thing to him: the animal was near played out. He took up the reins and began to lead the animal, hoping against hope that such a rest would be of benefit to it. But he also knew horses well enough to understand nothing short of several days and nights of rest in a comfortable stall with plenty of grain, fresh hay and water could help the pony much.

Melissa, discovering him once again on the ground, slid from her mount and fell in beside him. He glanced down to her and she smiled back with just her eyes. She, for one, was not giving up. As long as she could walk, she would not give in. He found some comfort in that, in her stalwart courage, and it stiffened his own resolve. And, unaccountably, it filled him with a pride for her.

He tried to figure ahead for the coming night. He needed to make plans, get things set in his mind so there would be no indecision and delay that would work in Harry Decket's favor. They should not risk stopping, he knew. Decket would permit no halting of the posse now that he was so close to his quarry. But could he and Melissa keep on going through the long night? They were tired already, without food and water, battling the everlasting wind that sapped at their strength. He had his doubts that they could go much further.

He began searching his mind for some idea, some strategy that would allow them to stop, to hide, perhaps, and let Decket and the posse bypass them. In the sweeping sand they could not easily be seen except at a close distance. But Decket would think of that; Decket, the tough and relentless, would take his extra precautions, expecting just such a move on their part. Right at that moment, Santell suspected, the sharp-faced marshal had his men spaced out at intervals determined by their ability to see the land on all sides and was marching across the prairie in a widely flung line that would not miss them.

No — halting on the empty flats would not work. As he fell to thinking again, the faint barking of a dog reached his ears. At first it meant nothing to him, just another sound borne on the rushing wind, and he walked slowly onward, wrestling with his problem. And then it came to him with sudden force.

A barking dog!

When there was a dog there also would be people. And that meant shelter. He came to a full stop, laying an arresting hand upon Melissa's shoulder to halt her.

"Listen!" He had to yell to make himself heard above the wind.

Melissa frowned. She pulled her shirt collar down to be able to hear better. It came again. She turned to him, her eyes alight. "A dog!"

He nodded. She had understood the meaning of it for them at once. "Coming from the south, I judge."

They waited out the sound again and when it came once more, they located its position as best they could; somewhere to the southward, perhaps a bit west, allowing for the wind.

Santell swung that direction at once, taking a route that was almost squarely right-angled to the route they had just traveled. If the storm would hold, if they could reach the dog and silence him, if it was a rancher's home or a homesteader's soddy or maybe a village of some sort, they might be safe. It seemed like a great number of *ifs* to Clay Santell but it was a good gamble to his way of thinking.

But they would have to find and quiet that dog. Otherwise Decket or one of his men would also hear and turn to locate the source. *Remember to shut up that dog,* he murmured to himself.

But the barking had ceased of its own accord before the hour was gone. They pressed on, guided by nothing more than jaded hope and a general sense of direction. The sun lowered, the day began to darken. Still the wind held, never lessening and showing little signs of doing so anytime in the near future.

They were both staggering slightly, almost dragging their reluctant horses behind them; they were too important to abandon, they were their only means for crossing the prairie miles to Splendor. Poor means, to be sure, but even this alternate system of walking and riding was better than being stranded on foot. They could at least hold their own against Harry Decket's constant, dogged stalking.

Santell halted suddenly. Directly ahead, not ten feet away, a broad shadow had appeared. He leaned forward, studying it through half-blinded eyes, making a closer examination. His tight nerves relaxed. It was a dark, mud-plastered hut with a lone glass window.

"A house!" Melissa cried at his elbow.

"Better than that," he replied, straining to see further along. "Looks like several. Maybe it's a village. Probably Mexican."

It made no difference. Here was human habitation; shelter, food, water, rest. And maybe a measure of security from the grim danger tagging at their heels.

12

Handing the reins of his horse to Melissa, Santell groped his way to the door of the adobe hut. He rapped sharply and presently it opened an inch or two. A dark face peered out at him.

"Alcalde? Usted?" he yelled, fumbling through his memory for the Spanish words that would direct him to the mayor or head of the village.

The door opened wider and a man stepped half-out and pointed to a house

146

farther along down the narrow street.

Santell said, *"Gracias, amigo,"* and turned away.

They made their way to the structure indicated, another low-roofed, mud brick house with a deeply recessed door. At Santell's knock, it opened at once and a portly Mexican presented himself.

"Hablo Inglés?" Santell asked, not trusting his abilities with the language much.

"*Si, yo hablo* — I speak English. A little. Some," the man replied with a toothy grin.

"You the *alcalde*, the mayor?"

"Yes. What you want?"

"Something to eat and drink."

The Mexican nodded. "You pay?"

"I can pay. *Tengo dinero.*"

The mayor's grin widened. He stepped back, holding open the door. With a low bow, he said, "*Buenas tardes,* welcome to the home of Mariano Lucero. Come to the inside. I call my woman. She fix for you the things to eat. *Chili, tamales, frijoles* . . . some corn."

"How about some coffee?" Santell suggested hopefully. "Some *café?*"

Lucero wagged his head. "No, *señor,* no *café. Chocolate.*"

The Mexican people seemed never to drink coffee. Their favored beverage, excluding wine, was chocolate, thick as soup.

Santell laid his hand on Lucero's thick shoulder as he started for the rear of the place. "The horses are tired and hungry. I want feed and water for them. Grain and hay and a place out of the wind for the night."

Lucero cocked his head. "I am a poor man, *señor*. I have no feed for horses. I would have to buy the hay and grain. You will pay?"

Santell reached into his pocket for a gold eagle. He handed it to the man. "This ought to pay for everything we get, horses and all."

Lucero beamed and nodded hastily. He half-turned and shouted something into the back rooms. A moment later his wife, a dark-faced squat woman, entered and looked at him wordlessly. He spoke rapidly to her in Spanish. When he was finished, she trundled about and shuffled off, still silent.

"You will eat soon, you and your wife," Lucero said. "I go now to care for the horses."

A thought came to Santell. "Where you going to put them?"

Lucero drew him to the window in the south wall. He pointed to a small shed back of the main house. "There is my poor stable, *señor*. But they will be warm and dry."

He wheeled about and pushed through the doorway into the wind. A moment later he passed the window leading the two exhausted horses.

Melissa had dropped to one of the low couches arranged against the wall, her shoulders slack with fatigue. She brushed at her lips with a square of lace-edged linen. "It's like heaven to be out of the wind," she murmured. "I feel gritty. Wonder if there's a place where I can wash up?"

"Could stand a little water in the right places myself," Santell agreed. "We're both covered with a pretty fair coat of sand. I'll see what I can do about it."

He went through the short hallway that led to the kitchen. Lucero's wife was preparing the meal. She paused to listen woodenly to his request, made in broken English and a smattering of Spanish. When he was finished she shook her head, her dark, flat face expressionless.

"No sabe," she said and went on with her work.

Santell tried again but got nowhere and after a time he returned to the front room and told of his failure to Melissa. "Lucero will be back soon. I'll talk to him."

"I guess it really doesn't matter," she said

with a sigh. "It's just good to be out of that wind. To sit down and not be walking."

He said solemnly, thinking of Harry Decket, "It's good to be alive."

He sank down on the other couch. She too, was thinking about Decket and Perrick and the other men of the posse. It had brought a flicker of alarm to her dark eyes and he was sorry he had mentioned it. He glanced about the room, snug against the howling sandstorm. Its walls were neatly whitewashed and adorned with religious paintings and drawings, all mounted in handmade frames. A crucifix hung in a small alcove below which a candle burned with a steady flame. There was a crudely built table, the two couches and a heavy chair. The floor was uncovered, the earth having been sprinkled and tamped and swept until it was hard as any timber. A clay pot of flowering geraniums stood in one window, their scarlet blossoms bright in the dimness. The place was spotless.

"Will we stay the night here?" Melissa asked.

Santell nodded. He was watching through the window, seeing Lucero emerge from the curtain of sand, followed by two other men carrying sacks of feed for the horses. "If Decket didn't get wise to our turning off, we should be able to stay until morning."

"You think he did?"

Santell shrugged his wide shoulders, the motion setting the couch to creaking. "Hard to say. He didn't see us swing out, I'm sure of that. And there'll be no tracks for that Indian to follow. If the storm holds he'll likely pass us by, thinking we're still somewhere ahead. If it stops, he'll catch on quick when he can't see us and start circling back. Sooner or later he'll come across this village."

Melissa's nerves suddenly shattered. "Decket! Decket! I hope I never again hear that awful name! It seems like he's been after us forever! Decket and that horrible, filthy Jake Perrick! Why does the good Lord let such people live?"

Santell came swiftly off the couch and crossed over to her. He sat down beside her and took her slim form into his arms, drawing her tightly against him. "Don't worry," he said softly. "It's almost over with now. I won't let them catch up to us." He stopped short, having a new thought. "Maybe it would be a good idea for you to stay here while I go on to Splendor. The Luceros could look after you a few days."

Without looking up she said, "No, I want to stay with you, Clay. I don't want to wait here. I feel safe — only with you."

Lucero came in at that moment, wiping his mouth with the back of his hand to remove the grit. "Do not think again of the horses, *señor.* They are most comfortable."

"Good," Santell said. "Any place we can wash up?"

Lucero nodded. He motioned for them to follow and took them on through the house to a small room on the back. A tin basin and a wooden bucket sat side by side on a low bench. Lucero stepped to an outside door and opened it. He pointed to a wood-framed well standing in the yard a dozen paces away.

"More water there," he said.

He produced a coarse towel from the kitchen and then he left them alone. Santell waited until Melissa had finished and then bathed his own face and hands. His chin and cheeks were so covered with whiskers that he could do little more than rinse the sand from them. But it did make him feel better.

"How is your side?" Melissa asked then when he was done. She did not wait for his answer but unbuttoned his shirt and made an inspection of the wound. It had bothered him little and, in truth, he had almost forgotten it.

"Doing all right," she announced. "We won't even bother to change the bandage."

"Had a mighty good doctor fix it up," Santell said jokingly with a wide grin.

She lifted her gaze to him. It was one of the few times she had seen or heard him gay. Her dark eyes were velvet soft. In the small anteroom, shut away from the howling storm, from everything and everyone, Clay Santell had a moment when words rushed to his lips. Unhampered by any thoughts of Eva and the past, he wanted to tell Melissa what she had come to mean to him and how empty the future would be after they reached Splendor and parted. But again some strong caution laid its restraint upon him, placed a wedge between them, checking his words. And in the next second the door opened.

Lucero said, "Eat now, my friends."

Melissa turned away from him, the light dying in her eyes. The magic of the moment was lost to them both. They followed Lucero into the kitchen and sat down at the square table with him and his wife. The food was good, although hot with chili seasoning. They ate heartily, surprised at their own hunger.

When they were through Santell said to Lucero, "How far to Texas? To the town

153

called Splendor?"

The Mexican thought for a moment. "A day by horse."

"Which way?"

"East. To the north a little, I think."

"Could you fix us up with a canteen of water and some grub — food, for the trip?"

Lucero nodded. "But you do not leave now?"

"In the morning."

"It will be ready," Lucero replied and conveyed his instructions to his wife in a torrent of Spanish.

It had been growing steadily darker. Lucero lit a lamp and guided them into the front room. The wind still moaned and tore at the adobe walls and the cold had increased. The Mexican offered Santell his tobacco and papers and the big man relaxed, skillfully spinning up a thin, brown shaft of yellow grains.

"What's the name of this village?" he asked, sitting down beside Melissa.

"*Villa de Lucero* — what you Americans call Luceroville. It was named for my father."

"Is there a place around where we can sleep? A hotel, an inn — a *posada?*"

Lucero's round face clouded. "This is a small place, *señor.* There is no inn. But I have a small hut in the back. It is my son's. He is gone. You are welcome to its use."

Santell hoped that it would be suitable for them. When Lucero had assumed, previously, that they were husband and wife he had made no correction, not attempting to explain they were only bound together by a common danger. It was a matter he would have difficulty in making clear to the Mexican. It was simpler to let it ride, acting the part as they had on the previous night. He remembered then the look on Melissa York's face; the quarters would have to be so arranged as they might rest comfortably — but well apart. He got to his feet.

"We'll go there now, *amigo*. We are both tired. *Muy cansado*."

Lucero grinned and nodded his understanding. He took them again through the warm little house, pungent with the odors of burning cedar wood, bubbling chili stewing on the makeshift stove, and some sort of sweet-smelling bread on. They went out to the smaller building near the stable where their horses were quartered.

It was much like the other, clean except for a fine film of dust that lay upon the furnishings. Lucero yanked the top blanket from the bed and shook it vigorously, raising a gray cloud in the room.

"It is not often used, this little house of my son's. He has been gone many days. I think he will never return but my wife says the good saints will bring him back to us. She prays and lights a candle for him every day. He is a good boy but sometimes he does very bad things."

"He'll be back some day," Melissa said kindly.

Santell said, "Now, about that grub and water for tomorrow, where will it be?" The easy, gay manner was gone from him now. He was once again grimly businesslike, alert to all dangers.

"It will be on the porch, where you washed," Lucero replied. He bowed his good night and backed into the yard. Santell followed.

He said, "There may be some men come here looking for me — us. Five men on horses. If they come, I'll take it as a good favor if you will tell them you have not seen us."

Lucero's dark face was still. "These men — are they the law, señor?"

Santell said frankly, "Yes," but he made no attempt to explain their trouble. That, too, was something he would never be able to get across, each being restricted by his meager knowledge of the other's language.

156

Lucero's face pulled into a frown. "I am a simple man — I dare not cause the law —"

Santell drew another gold coin from his pocket and offered it to the man. "Will this make you forget you saw us?"

Lucero grinned broadly. He took the coin. "I have not seen you, *señor,* or your beautiful *señora!*"

Santell delayed him with a firm grasp on his arm. "I can figure on that? We've got to get some sleep tonight. I don't want to worry about it."

Lucero looked injured. "My word is good, *señor.* You have it."

"Fine," Santell said, and turning, went back into the hut.

He closed the door and dropped the bar across it, locking it tight. It was full dark and he lit one of the candles lying on the shelf above the conical fireplace that bulged out of one corner of the room. With Melissa sitting on the edge of the bed, he made a tour of their quarters, familiarizing himself with it, locating the windows, searching for another door.

"Only one," he stated finally. "If we have to get out of here in a hurry, it'll have to be by the way we came in. Don't like that much."

"How about the windows?"

Santell shook his head. "All too small. I could get you through any of them but they won't fit me. One good thing, there's one in each wall. At least we can see out in all four directions."

He set the candle back on the shelf and again made the rounds of the room, this time drawing closed the thick, woven curtains. He moved then to the center of the small quarters and let his eyes run over the furnishings: the bed; a single, stiff-backed, homemade chair; a chest with five drawers, the front of which was badly scarred. There were several religious prints on the white-washed walls and the inevitable crucifix in its niche. Unconsciously, he had reverted to the pattern of the past, to the only Santell Melissa York knew. He stood there now, poised like a crouched listening cat, preparing for any emergency. He knew exactly where each item lay. Awakening suddenly he would make no mistakes in their fight for survival.

And then he relaxed. "We'd better get all the rest we can," he murmured, moving toward the chest. A heavy pair of shearing clippers of the type commonly found around sheep camps lay upon its top. "Tomorrow could be a tough day. If you'll give me one of those blankets, I'll roll up here on the floor. The bed's yours."

He saw relief again break across Melissa's features and it angered him. She had failed utterly to understand that she was safe with him! That he had no real interest in her other than to deliver her safely to Splendor where she could obtain further help in getting to Missouri. Oh, there was no denying she was an attractive woman, even a beautiful one if she had the chance to fix up a bit; but she made it plain how she felt about men in general and it matched exactly with his feelings toward all women. So they were even. And that's the way he wanted it to stay. Santell's thoughts came to a full halt. Somehow he was no longer convincing himself with such arguments; somehow they no longer rang true.

Melissa had risen and pulled off two of the thick woolen covers. "I'll have plenty," she said. "Use one for a mat. That floor will be hard."

Santell fashioned his pallet and sat down to remove his boots.

Melissa stretched out on the bed, sighing at its deep comfort. "This time tomorrow night," she murmured dreamily, "we will be safe. Decket and Jake Perrick will be just a bad memory. One we can forget."

"Hope so," Santell replied, unfolding his

long frame and pulling the blanket around him. "If we can keep out of their way and the horses will hold out, we'll make it. With a little good luck," he amended.

She considered his words. After a time she said, "When it's all over with Clay, what happens to you? Where are you headed?"

She waited for him to answer and when he did not she raised her head and glanced down at him. He was already sleeping soundly. Studying him for a full minute, she came soundlessly off the bed and bending over him, kissed him lightly on the mouth. Immediately she was back under her covers.

13

A man's dreams, like his thoughts, are his own, and Clay Santell found no comfort in the visionary wanderings of his mind while he slept on the hard floor of Lucero's hut.

The sharp, gimlet-eyed face of Harry Decket was everywhere, peering at him from behind the tall pines of the forests, the scrubby cedars of the lesser hills, from huge boulders — from the corners of Luceroville's houses even. He was there in the low sink holes of the prairies; he was everywhere. Santell found he could not flee although he tried desperately, always pushing Melissa York ahead of him to keep her from harm's way.

Every escape route was blocked and Splendor, where safety lay, was a lofty, ivory-capped citadel isolated atop an unreachable hill. And through it all, back in the shadows lurked the gross shape of Jake Perrick, watching and waiting for a moment when, unguarded, Melissa would fall victim to his clutches.

He came awake with a start, sweating freely. The moaning of the wind had faded and this at once filled him with alarm. He threw aside the blanket and bounded to the window near the door. Outside the prairie was bathed in a glowing, silver starshine, almost bright as day.

A man astride a rangy horse was at the back of Lucero's house, guarding that exit with a drawn gun. It was Tex London. He knew then what had awakened him. It was the pounding around at the front, the insistent hammering on the door. That would be Decket or Perrick summoning the Mexican for questioning. He saw movement then in the narrow, crooked street. Two others, Charley Ironhead and Sam Cunningham, were walking their horses slowly toward the next house, already beginning their door-to-door search, not waiting for

Lucero to make his answers.

Santell moved quickly. He shook Melissa gently by the shoulder and when she opened her eyes, he whispered, "They're here. We've got to run for it!"

She sat up at once and he turned to draw on his boots, frantically plotting escape. The single entrance was out of the question, opening as it did directly into the small yard where Tex London waited. He could try to slip out and pull the tall deputy from his saddle and put him out of action the best way possible. But there was bound to be some sort of resulting commotion and in the early morning quiet it surely would be heard by Decket and the others.

He wished now he had remembered to ask Lucero if he had a gun he might buy. He had noticed none, no weapon of any sort in the house except for an ancient Mexican cavalry officer's sword hanging on one of the walls. Lucero had worn no pistol. Likely he owned no gun of any sort but Santell still regretted that he had not asked.

Fully dressed now, he stood in the center of the little room and considered their position. They had to get out of the hut quickly; the search would soon reach them and there was no telling how long Mariano Lucero, faced by the combined pressures and threats of both Decket and Perrick, would hold out before he was forced to tell what he knew.

Melissa was ready to go. He pointed to the window and she had her look at the deputy, understanding at once the gravity of their situation. He turned then to the rear window, farthest from the door, which looked out upon the flats behind the village. It was a simple wood frame-and-glass affair, set in the adobe wall with mud mortar. It was stationary and did not swing open. Santell gave it a brief examination and then snatched up the wool shears off the chest. They would make a good tool with which to dig.

He began chipping away the mortar below the window's sill. It came out easily and in a few minutes he was able to lift the sash in his hands and set it aside. Cool, prairie air rushed in, sharpening his senses. The opening was still too small for him and he set to work removing a row of the adobe bricks. When that was done he slipped silently through to the outside. Reaching back, he picked Melissa up and lifted her after him.

He breathed easier. At least they were on the outside, out of the hut that had become a deadly trap. But they were a long way from escape and from the horses in the stable only a few feet away across the open yard.

Motioning for Melissa to remain at the corner of the hut, he worked his way along the side to where he could see Lucero's house.

Tex London was still there. A murmur was coming from the front. Charley Ironhead and Cunningham were out of sight, somewhere down the street. He paused then, again calculating his chances for sneaking up behind London and silencing the redhead with a single, well directed blow. The odds were too great, and for the second time he discarded the thought. Even if he managed to subdue London without his making an outcry, a shying, frightened horse was certain to arouse suspicion. It was no good that way.

How then to reach the stable?

Once they got across the empty yard and gained the barn, they could ready the horses and wait their chances to make a run for it. London would leave his post eventually, unless of course Lucero broke down and told Decket where the fugitives were hiding. Even so that would not work out too badly; Decket would surround the hut where they had been and while the posse was doing this, he and Melissa might be able to slip away unnoticed. Getting into the stable was the problem.

He crawled noiselessly back to where Melissa crouched. "We've got to get to those horses," he said in a low voice. "Means crossing that yard, right out there in the open. Good chance for London or one of the others to see us. Not going to be easy."

"Whatever you say," she murmured. "I'm ready."

He gave her a brief, hard grin. "Could be the last walk we'll ever take. Any of them sees us, they'll start shooting. They won't bother to pick their target."

"But it's our only chance — and we might make it."

He said, "Sure."

"Then I'm ready."

An idea came to him then. "No use both of us taking the chance at the same time. Be better if we go one after the other. Less apt to wake Tex. You wait here. I'll get across the yard to the stable and when it looks clear again, I'll give you a signal."

She was immediately suspicious of his plan and made her whispered protest. "You're doing that to protect me! You're afraid they may start shooting and I'll get hurt. I won't have it that way! I'm as much to blame for our being here, trapped like this, as anything. I won't let you take all these chances just for my sake!"

"You'll do exactly what I tell you to do!" Santell replied harshly. "Doing it my way is the best. He looked away from her, throwing his glance toward the village, dim and shadowy in the early morning hour. "What makes you think I'm giving any special thought to you? This is just the best way to handle it."

She stared at his sun-blackened profile for a moment. "All right," she said. "Only — be careful, Clay."

He turned his attention back to the street near the house. Still no signs of Cunningham or the Indian. That bothered him most of all. At any moment either of them might turn up and to see him crossing the yard would be easy for anyone looking in that general direction. He swung his attention to Lucero's house. A lamp had been lit, its weak, yellow light showing in the glass square where the red geraniums had been. That would mean Decket and probably Jake Perrick were inside now. London still sat his horse, his shoulders slack, chin dropped to his chest. Decket had apparently kept them all in the saddle during the entire night. He turned to Melissa.

"Watch for my signal. When I give it, come fast and quiet."

She nodded. He crouched and then, with

a final sweeping survey of the street, of Lucero's house and the yard, he moved off for the stable. He kept low, not running but walking in long strides. It was a good twenty-five feet to the barn, and for that entire distance he was plainly visible from Lucero's or from the street. Or by Tex London if he chanced to rouse and look back over his shoulder. It required only seconds to cover the distance but it seemed like ages to Clay Santell. When he reached the half-open door of the stable, he stepped inside and leaned up against the rough wall of the structure, drawing his first full breath since he had left the corner of the hut.

He went back to the opening and glanced out into the starlit night. The street was still empty, stone quiet. London had not moved and the pale flare of the lamp was still mirroring against Lucero's window. He looked toward the hut. Melissa was a dark shadow where he had left her. Waiting out another long minute to be certain, he lifted his arm and motioned for her to come. She did so, running across the hard pack as swift and silent as a deer.

After she was safely inside, he drew her back into the darkness, leaving the door ajar for a quick exit if it should become necessary. He located the bridles for the horses.

No actual plan for escape was in his mind at that time; he was meeting each problem as it presented itself, doing the things that had to be done, one at a time. When the ponies were ready, he made a tour of the stables. It was small, very little larger than Lucero's hut. But it did have a rear door.

Hope soared through Santell when he made that discovery. He cleared away the scatter of trash that lay piled up against its base and drew it open. It was suspended by leather hinges, improvised from old harness straps and it sagged, setting up a loud scuffing noise as it scraped across the floor. Santell silently cursed his own carelessness and, lifting the stab, opened it wide.

He was aware then of Melissa at his elbow, touching his wrist. "That noise! London heard it. He's coming around the side to look."

He nodded and pushed her back into the deep shadows. Taking a stand just within the now-open door, he listened. The slow, cautious step of Tex London was audible along the far wall. The deputy had judged the noise to have originated behind the stable and was coming to investigate. Santell glanced hurriedly about looking for a suitable weapon. There was no length of board, no tool such as a shovel or pick or axe handy. He knotted his fists. It would have to be with them.

London reached the corner and paused. Santell could hear the regular drawing of his breath, plain in the tension-filled hush. For a moment he thought Tex had satisfied his suspicions and decided to return to the yard but in the next instant he heard his nearer step. Santell drew himself up against the door and set himself for the attack. It would have to be fast, brutal and quiet.

London's shape suddenly blocked the doorway, closing off the bright, silver fog of starlight. Santell struck out with all his power, straight at the redhead's jaw. London dodged quickly and Santell's driving fist caught him in the neck, missing its target. It knocked the man down but not unconscious. Santell was on him in a lunge through the doorway, reaching with both hands. He must not allow Tex to cry out. They crashed together and London struggled wildly to get from beneath Santell.

Santell batted his arms away and hammered at the deputy's face, his head, eyes, ears. His breath was coming in short gasps and pain was shooting through him where London had slammed into his wounded side. The deputy's clutching fingers found his hair and jerked hard. It pulled Santell from his position of advantage, tipping him sideways. But as he fell, he locked his hands about London's neck. They began to thresh about on the ground, rolling back and forth, clawing, heaving, striking with short savage blows.

Santell was the first to break clear. He bounded to his feet, legs quivering from his straining efforts. Tex London was mere seconds slower but it was enough. Santell caught him on the point of the chin with a right hand that traveled a long way. The blow cracked like a dry branch underfoot. London's arms flew wide. His head bobbed to the back of his shoulders and his long body went stiff. He dropped heavily to the ground.

Santell staggered back, sucking for wind. He leaned against the barn. After a moment he brushed the hair from his eyes with the back of his skinned hand. He located his hat and stooping, retrieved it, mechanically knocking dust off it against his knee. He looked around, half-expecting to see Decket or one of the posse members, drawn by the noise of the conflict, standing there waiting for him. He saw only Melissa.

She was in the doorway, the horses ready behind her. There was a light in her eyes, a bright excitement that reflected both her relief and pride in his victory. She laid the reins to his horse in his hand. Still short of breath, he pulled himself upon the back of his mount. She was already seated and waiting for him when he looked again.

"Which way, Clay?"

He ducked his head toward the west, toward the mountains from which they had come. "That way. For a time. Until we can safely circle the village. Then east."

Melissa raised no question but started immediately. His horse fell in behind hers. They had covered no more than a dozen steps when she halted.

Santell glanced up quickly. "What is it?"

"The Indian — Charley Ironhead. He's up there just ahead. Waiting for us!"

14

Santell slipped from his horse and crept softly ahead, keeping to the crumpled wall of a deserted hut. The silver glow of stars lay across the prairie and it was almost as if it were daytime with the sun flooding down in full force. He reached the end of the ruin and halted. Cautiously raising his head he let his gaze rest upon the lone rider sitting somewhat apart from the village. He was stationed at a point where he could see anyone who approached or attempted to leave.

Melissa was right. It was Charley Ironhead. Santell had thought him somewhere in the village, but somehow he had circled, unseen, back through the houses and had taken up a post at that extreme corner. Then Cunningham, logically, was guarding the opposite end of Luceroville.

Santell studied the hunched figure with its incongruous forage cap perched high on the head. The Indian was in a position to see any move they made once they left the squat adobe buildings of the village. There was no way, so far as he could see, around him. Santell turned and made his way back to Melissa. Saying nothing, he took up the reins of her horse and, with his own mount at her side, retreated as quietly as possible toward the stable. When they were beyond all possibility of being overheard by Charley Ironhead, he stopped.

"We'll try the other direction. South."

Tex London lay where he had fallen, face down. But he would be out for only a short time longer, and Santell wanted to be a far distance from the village by the time the tall deputy regained consciousness and set up the alarm. They moved by him, Melissa still on her pony, Santell walking ahead, leading the way. They passed behind the next adobe hut, working deeper into the settlement. Suddenly a woman's anguished scream broke through the early morning air. Santell hauled up short.

It had come from Mariano Lucero's house, as near as he could tell. Probably the Mexican's wife. It could mean only one thing: Decket and Perrick had tossed away the velvet glove in their dealings with the man and his wife and now, in their unholy zeal to find Santell and Melissa, were resorting to brute force. Anger rushed through him; his quarrel with the two men was his own; he could match them and take all they had to give but when they turned their brutality and vindictive hate upon harmless people such as the Luceros, it rankled him beyond reason.

The cry did not come again. Lucero's wife had been struck by either Perrick or Decket for some reason, Santell guessed. He wondered then what Decket and Perrick were doing to Lucero. How long could he hold out? Would he be able to stand by his word and keep a tight mouth or would the punishment eventually loosen his tongue?

He continued on, having his dark thoughts about the marshal and his companion. The huts of the village were more numerous in the center of the settlement, scattered helter-skelter without regard to plan or the narrow, winding street that wove through them. It was characteristic of the Mexican people that they always built several smaller huts for their offspring on the back of the family lot, thus giving each child a home of his own when he was grown. The result was that one small, half-acre plot might have from four to eight separate dwellings built on it at various angles and points.

Working among these, moving in and out, Santell finally was able to cross over to the opposite side of the village some distance below Mariano Lucero's home.

Pushing on through, they broke out onto the prairie once again. Here Santell halted, keenly worried about the deputy, Sam Cunningham. He would, in all likelihood, be guarding the village at this far end just as the Indian was doing the other. But at which corner? Would he be watching the flats that lay between Luceroville and the mountains over which they had come the day before or would he confine his vigilance to the east, to the prairie that yet lay between them and the town of Splendor?

Leaving Melissa with the horses, he followed out the shadows until he was standing at last at the extreme south end of the village. Cunningham was not to be seen. This disturbed Santell. It was better to find the man and know where he was than to be completely in the dark about him. It was no good, never knowing where he was, if he might be waiting around a corner, gun drawn, ready to shoot. He returned to Melissa.

"Can't spot Cunningham," he said in a low voice. "Figured he would be at this end of the town but I don't see him. We'll have to risk bumping into him."

He looked out across the prairie, toward the east. A darker, shadowed strip lay parallel to the village some hundred yards or so distant. A swale, or an arroyo bed. It was an answer to their needs. Again leaving Melissa with the horses, he moved off to investigate. It was exactly what he had hoped for — a deep, long-running arroyo they could use to leave the village without being seen.

He hurried back to the girl and, taking up the reins, led the horses down into the wash. It was steep-sided and he had to hunt along its bank for a good hundred yards before he could find a spot where the ponies could work their way down without falling. A cool determination had settled within Santell's mind. Here was a ready-made escape route, barred possibly at the far end by Cunningham. But that matter could be dealt with later. At that moment the screams of Mariano Lucero's wife still echoed in his ears and there was something he had to do about that. There was a strong possibility that stopping now would endanger their own chances for escape but he wasn't considering that. He was growing tired of the everlasting running anyway and it was time he struck back even if in a minor way. Lucero had befriended him and for that he was being badly manhandled by Decket and Perrick. Santell would stop that.

But first there was the matter of Melissa's safety. He wanted that assured. He handed her the reins. "Wait here for me. Keep close to the bank, under the brush. I've got to go back."

She met his eyes questioningly. "Lucero?"

He nodded, grateful for her understanding. "It won't take long. Give me fifteen minutes and if I'm not back, you ride on. Follow out this arroyo and then turn east when you get to its end. You'll reach Splendor that way. You might leave my horse."

Melissa shook her head. "I'll wait here, no matter how long it takes. And if you aren't back, I'll come looking for you."

"And walk right into Jake Perrick's hands?

No, you leave if I don't get back. Fifteen minutes and then be on your way."

She studied his uptilted face for a moment. "Don't worry about me, Clay. Just you be careful. And come back."

"I'll do that," he replied with a grin and turned back to the arroyo's side and climbed from its depth.

He worked his way back through the houses quietly, still uncertain and disturbed about the unknown whereabouts of Sam Cunningham. The pattern of events had taken on more definite shape in the past few minutes. Decket and his posse had come into the village much as he and Melissa had. They had stopped at the first hut to make their inquiry and the man there likely had directed them to Lucero's place.

Thus Decket was certain Lucero knew of Santell's presence. That he was sure Clay was in or close by Lucero's residence was further proved by Tex London's steady watch at the rear of the structure. He wondered then if the deputy had recovered yet, if he had returned to his post. If so, he apparently had raised no alarm, preferring to keep his defeat to himself rather than lay himself open to censure and ridicule by Decket and the others. Thinking of the deputy, Santell had a moment of amusement; it had been London who was standing at the back door of the restaurant in Sutterville. He had run the man down like a stampeding steer. And now, here in the shadows of a Mexican village they had again met violently. It seemed they were fated to tangle at every opportunity.

At the end of a small pole corral he halted, spending a precious minute to listen. There was nothing on the still air as he moved on, his thoughts again returning to the question of Cunningham's post. It had become a burning issue with him, a key to the ultimate escape of Melissa and himself. He could be at the extreme north end backing up Charley Ironhead or he could be searching the village, hut by hut. He could be no more than a step away at that very moment, just waiting for Santell to round a corner and come into the open. Or he could be waiting patiently at the upper end of the deep arroyo just beyond the village, figuring Santell and Melissa would employ that as their avenue of flight; that was assuming they had also discovered the wash.

He stopped directly opposite Lucero's house. He had thought of no plan for attack; he actually had no mind to attack in that sense of the word but meant merely to draw the lawman's attention to him and thus detract it from Lucero. When that was accomplished he would try to return to the arroyo, following a devious route so as to not lead them to where Melissa waited with the horses.

He wished then he had told Melissa to ride further up the wash, at least for a mile or two. She would be that much safer at that distance from the village when trouble started. But he knew she would not have done so; she was stubborn about such things and somehow it gave him a good feeling to know she was waiting for him, counting on him, keeping his horse there ready for instant use.

He came to the last houses and crowded up against the wall of one. Mariano Lucero's place was straight across, its door standing wide open. The low, muffled sobbing of Lucero's wife came from somewhere in the darkened interior. Two horses stood near the corner of the building, their heads hanging wearily. Sam Cunningham was not to be seen and again Santell wondered about the man. He needed desperately to know just where the deputy was at that moment.

There were sounds of scuffling coming from within Lucero's, followed at once by the meaty thud of a blow struck hard. Lucero's wife cried out and someone crashed against the door's frame. Lucero reeled into view and dropped in a heap at the edge of the street. Decket came out, following closely. Jake Perrick was at the marshal's heels.

Decket was trembling with frustrated rage. He drew back his booted foot and kicked Lucero savagely in the ribs. The Mexican groaned and writhed away, sprawling in the dust.

"Get him on his feet!"

Perrick leaned forward, grasped Lucero under the shoulders and dragged him to an upright position. Doubling the man's arms behind his back, he thrust him at the marshal, a suspended target.

"What about it, Lucero? Where'd you hide Travers?"

The Mexican shook his head wearily. "Travers — I do not know that name, *señor.* I never hear it before."

Decket struck him a vicious crack on the face. Lucero's head wobbled grotesquely.

"This here is sure one Mex that can take it," Jake Perrick remarked with a hint of admiration in his tone.

"He'll be a dead Mex if he don't talk pretty quick!" Decket snapped. "Cut out the stallin', Lucero. We know Travers was here. A big man with a girl. Your *paisano* down the street said so. Said he sent them to see you. Now, either you tell me what you did with them or I'll beat it out of you and your old woman!"

"No sabe," Lucero moaned. *"No sabe* Travers."

Decket's balled fist drove hard into the man's unprotected belly. Wind gushed from his flared mouth. He buckled forward to the dust. *"No, señor, no! Por favor!"* he pleaded.

Anger surged through Clay Santell like a roaring tidal wave. His hand dropped to the gun at his side — and came away. It was empty but there was a chance he could bluff with it. But the pistol was gone. He must have lost it during the fight with Tex London. He no longer cared. His determination to help the beaten Mexican was too strong.

Keeping in the deep shadows along the wall of the hut, he glanced over his shoulder, planning his movements. He would have to move fast now. He swung his attention back to the street, to the three men. Lucero was still folded forward, supported only by Perrick's locking grasp of his arms.

Santell took a step forward. "Decket — here!" he said loudly.

The marshal whirled. Perrick released his hold on Lucero and grabbed at his rifle leaning against Lucero's wall. Santell in three long steps had spun and reached the end of the hut and rushed around its corner. Perrick's pistol blasted the night but Santell was already running, dodging behind the next house.

He heard a horse pounding in from the northeast edge of the village. Cunningham! It was a good thing after all that Melissa had not gone on ahead; the deputy might have seen her. He could hear Perrick and Decket trotting along the far side of the building near which he stood. He heard them stop when they came to its end and were faced with an empty alleyway.

"Where's that damned Indian?" Decket's voice was a harsh, impatient bellow.

"He's comin'," Perrick's slower tones replied. "Here's Sam now. You seen Tex, Sam?"

"Ain't seen nobody," Cunningham answered dourly.

"Get off that horse," Decket snapped. "Travers is on foot around here somewhere close. Hiding behind one of these shacks."

Santell slipped softly along through the scatter of houses, keeping always to the deep shade caused by the fading starlight. The gun's crashing had awakened the entire village. He saw doors open cautiously an inch or so and then swiftly close. He moved on, working his way in and out, trying to keep the sounds of the pursuit fixed in his mind. He thought mainly now of Charley Ironhead. The Indian could travel fast and soft as a cat. The others were clumsy, the scuffing of their boots easily broadcasting their actions.

He crossed the village, purposely leading the posse away from the eastern side, from the arroyo where Melissa and the horses waited. When he reached a corner not far from Lucero's house, he pulled up. Decket and the other men, excluding possibly Charley Ironhead, were well behind him. He stalled until they were within easy hearing distance and then drove his booted foot against a pile of chopped kindling wood and moved on quickly.

Perrick's voice instantly shouted, "There he is! Over here, boys! Over here!"

Santell watched from the deep cover of a shed as the marshal and Perrick came running across the small, open plaza toward the sound. A moment later Cunningham and the Indian appeared, breaking out of the huts a short distance further down. Santell faded back along the shed, ducked behind a house in which a small child was crying fretfully and came out at Lucero's stable. The yard was empty and he raced across it to the back of Lucero's house. Circling that, he reached the street. Decket and the others were searching the grounds some fifty yards below.

He paused at the corner of Lucero's house and threw a cautious glance down the silent street. The Mexican was the only person visible. He sat on the ground still clutching his middle with spread-eagled hands. Santell moved up beside him. Lucero looked up quickly, terror springing alive in his dark eyes. When he recognized Santell he smiled weakly.

"*Muchas gracias,*" Santell said in a low voice. "I'm sorry I brought trouble to your house, my friend. I'm going now. They won't bother you any more."

"*Es nada,*" Lucero wheezed softly. "My word has been kept. *Adios. Vaya con Dios.*"

"*Adios,*" Santell replied and crossed the street quickly. Somewhere down in the village he thought he could hear a horse walking but it was in the wrong direction to be coming from Decket and the posse members. He decided it was some other sound. He could plainly hear the marshal and his men over behind Lucero's. He hurried on.

In a few moments time he was lost in the maze of huts.

15

At the pistol's crack Shotgun Travers was awake and on his feet. He came off the crude cot in a single, automatic bound, a man who lived by the gun and whose reflexes responded instinctively to the sound of gunfire. Except for his boots he was fully dressed. He had reached first for the old Henry repeating rifle he had bargained Copio Gonzales out of, secondly for his boots. He was standing there in the darkness of the small, low-ceilinged room listening when Gonzales, clad only in his underwear, entered bearing a sickly burning candle.

"Somebody shoot!" Gonzales said.

"Put out that light!" Travers growled.

Gonzales snuffed the candle obediently. Travers moved to the low door, opened it cautiously and peered out. It was early, not later than four or four-thirty, he guessed, and the village was still a contrast of starlit open areas and darkly shadowed corners. He could see nobody but he could hear voices in the distance. They were coming from the far end of the settlement. He slipped into the narrow passageway that ran along Gonzales' hut and moved a dozen yards or so toward the confusion. But he still could see no one.

"Get off that horse! Travers is on foot around here somewhere close. Hiding behind one of these shacks!"

Travers did not need to see the speaker. He well knew that voice — Harry Decket. He pivoted on his heel and strode quickly back to Copio Gonzales' place. How Decket had discovered he was holed up in Luceroville was a puzzle — one he had no time to solve. He had to get out of there fast.

Gonzales was standing in the doorway when he reached the hut. He shouldered him aside roughly. "Got to hightail it out o' here. Get my horse, Copio."

"Who is it, kid?" the Mexican asked.

"Decket. That damned marshal. Hurry it up!"

Gonzales said no more. His scarecrow figure faded into the gloom, heading for the small shed where Travers' horse was stabled. Travers checked the rifle. It was old and rusty but the action was pretty good. He had only thirteen cartridges, all that Copio had, and he now fed them carefully into the long magazine, being careful in the darkness not to get one of them reversed.

He swore softly to himself. Decket would

never take him alive again, he promised himself that much. And if he got half a chance he was going to settle up old scores with the marshal. If he lived to be a hundred, he would never forget those weeks in that Arizona jail! And then that ride up to Colorado. He owed Decket plenty — a thousand things that needed paying back.

There was a sound outside. He stepped warily to the door, the rifle held in the crook of his thick arm. It was Gonzales with his horse. He finished the loading and stepped outside. The reins in his left hand, the gun in his right, he swung up. Astride the big bay horse, he did not slip the rifle in its boots but kept it, cradling it in his arm.

"*Adios*, kid," Gonzales murmured in his thick, soft voice.

"*Adios*, Copio. See you in Texas."

He turned due east through the village. The noise was still coming from the other end of the settlement and Travers grinned, a hard, wicked grin that stretched his lips tight over his teeth. Whoever it was who was drawing the marshal's attention had done him a favor. They had been decoyed away from his hiding place. But that wouldn't hold for long. Eventually Decket would discover his error and then a house-by-house search would begin.

He wondered how Decket had known he was in Luceroville, considering the question for the second time. He had figured it a perfect hideout. No one had seen him arrive he was certain. He had waited until full dark, until the lamps were all out, and then slipped into the village and gone straight to Gonzales' place. He knew the Mexican had not talked. He had known him for years, since back in San Luis, and Copio could be trusted. No, it was just Harry Decket. The damned, skinny little runt was part bloodhound.

He reached the edge of the settlement. Ahead lay a fairly open field area followed by a band of trees and yet shadowed brush. He halted there studying it, not liking it much. He would be in plain sight, right out in an open field, while he was crossing. Listening, then, he could hear a voice shouting. It was not Decket's voice; it did not carry the impatient edge that distinguished the marshal's. One of the posse members, likely.

So Decket and his men were still in the far corner of the village! Their voices told him that. A measure of curiosity and a bit of the man's reckless daring pushed to the fore. He'd like to have a look at what was causing all the ruction. He'd like to see this decoy, whoever he was, who was pulling Decket and the posse off his back. And he would like to have another squint at the marshal himself. It would make a damn good story he could tell in the Texas saloons; how he had sat back on his horse and watched Decket and his posse work over some other poor devil they thought was him.

He clucked the bay, a good horse Gonzales had provided for him and in fine condition after its rest. He skirted along the edge of the huts, never relaxing his vigilance but enjoying the moments of his little victory over Harry Decket.

Reaching the last of the houses, he paused momentarily. There were two or three yet between him and the activities of the posse. He turned the bay and rode deliberately toward the noise. He halted suddenly, just at the edge of the street, the rifle coming up swiftly. A man, it looked like one of the Mexicans, sat in the dust, hands holding his belly like he had been shot through. Apparently he wasn't the one they were now after. Just some unlucky Mex that had got in the way. It wasn't his worry.

Travers turned his attention back to the hunt. It seemed to be taking place somewhere on the other side of the street. For a time he sat there and pondered. It wouldn't be smart to cross the street, he decided. A man was a fool to take too much of a gamble. Anyway, he had a good enough story to tell. True, he hadn't actually seen the marshal and his men doing their looking for him but it was almost as good. They weren't more than a hundred yards away and that was close enough for the story.

He came to a sudden alert. He had caught movement along the side of a hut, the one behind the injured Mexican. Quickly but quietly he backed the bay away from the corner. When he was a safe distance withdrawn, he wheeled him around. He held the horse to a walk until he had reached the village limits and then increased the pace to a fast run.

He crossed the open field somewhat north of the settlement and when he reached the dark band of brush the horse was moving at a ground-covering gallop. The big bay horse was enjoying the run after a day and a half of rest.

Five minutes like this, Travers thought, and I'll be so far ahead of Decket he'll never catch up. Not until I reach Texas anyway and then it won't matter. I don't give a hoot about him once I'm there. He can't touch me there.

He was still thinking of Texas, of the

freedom awaiting him there, of the good times he would have, when the bay broke through the fringe of brush bordering an arroyo and went plunging down onto the rock and gravel.

16

Santell reached the arroyo and slipped into its depths. He was somewhat north of Melissa. Keeping close to the ragged, weed-grown bank, he backtracked until he made out the bulky outlines of the two horses and her slender shape standing nearby. She had drawn into a clump of bush to mask her position. She saw him approaching but waited until she was certain before she moved out to greet him, a glad smile on her lips.

"I heard shooting," she said at once, her voice tight with anxiety. "Are you all right?"

"All right," he replied. "No time left. We've got to run for it!"

He took the reins from her hands and started along the arroyo, walking in his customary long strides. Melissa, at his side, was hard pressed, half-running to match his pace.

"Where are they now?" she managed after a time.

"Behind Lucero's, I reckon. Still looking for me. I had to show myself. A fool thing to do but I had to do it."

"I know," she answered.

"If I'd had a gun, I would have killed that Decket, marshal or not, right there in the street!" he said then, his voice savage and furious. "Perrick was holding Lucero while Decket beat him."

"If you had your gun —" she echoed. "Didn't you?"

"Lost it. Probably back there when I tangled with Tex London. But it wasn't any good to me. Empty."

"You've got shells in your belt!"

"Wrong size. That was really Perrick's gun. I took it back there in the canyon. I used it when we were running for the trees. I didn't know it was a smaller caliber than mine until I tried to reload it."

He came to a halt, laying his free hand upon her slim shoulder. For a time he listened, something having caught up his keen senses and setting alert some caution within him. But after a bit he was satisfied and they pushed on, moving at a fast, almost desperate walk.

"Maybe just as good I didn't have a gun," he said coming back to the subject. "Had I blasted into Decket and Perrick, I would have had all the rest of them on my neck."

"How about Lucero?"

"I got them off him. He took a bad beating."

"I'm glad — that they'll leave him be now," she replied. "He was our friend when we needed one."

There was only the muted sound of the horses' hoofs in the soft sand for a space and then Santell, his voice grim, said, "I'll pay Harry Decket back for that one day! He'll draw interest for every time he hit Lucero."

They were keeping to the center of the arroyo's bed, away from the larger rocks and gravel that bound the edges. It was quieter there and it permitted Santell a better view of the outside country. He slowed the pace, dropping to a walk. "No talking, not for a while," he said. "We're about opposite Lucero's place."

Melissa nodded and they continued on, still walking, sparing the horses. And Santell had another reason; he feared their increased height, should they mount the animals, might be seen above the level of the arroyo's rim and possibly draw attention. They maintained a steady pace, spurred by the certain knowledge that safety lay only in distance, that Decket's relentless search would eventually reach to the arroyo and their tracks in the soft bottom would be plain and easy to read.

They came to the extreme corner of the village and Santell, thinking then of Tex London asked, "You see anybody while you were waiting?"

"No one. Why?"

"At first I couldn't locate Cunningham. But he showed up when the trouble started. He had been sitting it out somewhere along here. Then I couldn't find Tex."

"You don't think he's still there behind the barn — maybe dead?"

He shook his head. "I didn't hit him that hard. Anyway, his horse was gone from behind Lucero's."

"Then maybe he's somewhere ahead of us?"

Santell said, "Could be. Everyone showed up there to help nail me but Tex. Could be Decket put him out here at the end of the village and told him to stay put, just in case we got away from them. Decket's pretty cagey that way."

The arroyo began to deepen. Santell increased his vigilance, watching far ahead, searching along the banks and as far out on the flats as he could see. Once they halted and he crawled to the rim of the wash to study the surrounding country. When he returned he seemed relieved, apparently satisfied with what he had seen.

"We'll try riding now," he said moving over to help her mount.

She was still thinking about the missing gun. "It's odd," she began and stopped. A small cry wrenched itself from her throat. "Clay! Somebody's coming!"

It was almost a sob. A tight, hopeless, weary protest against the poor luck that seemed to plague them at every turn. Santell said nothing. Stepping forward, he grabbed her by the waist and swung her from the horse. With his arm still around her, they ducked into the deep shadows of a large mesquite bush. Motioning for her to remain there, he wormed his way up the side of the arroyo and saw the rider just emerging from a thicket at the edge of the settlement.

It was Sam Cunningham. The deputy rode slowly toward them, apparently not having seen them yet. He halted, turning his head as he swept the surrounding flats with his eyes. Santell felt around through the mesquite for a club or a rock that would serve as a weapon. If the man came any closer he would spot the horses. And that would bring him on in. Santell felt Melissa thrust a smooth, round stone into his groping hand.

Cunningham had probably been dispatched by Harry Decket immediately after they failed to find him in the huts near Lucero's place. He would suspect some sort of ruse and throw out precautionary measures. Probably another of the posse members was directly across, somewhere near that point where Charley Ironhead had been posted earlier.

He felt Melissa shudder slightly. She had crawled up from the depths of the bush and now was lying close beside him. The strain was getting to be too much for her; he was glad they were no further from Splendor than they actually were. Cunningham, satisfied with his survey, clucked his horse into motion and came on forward a few more steps. Santell tensed himself for action. Then Cunningham slowly circled away, doubling back for the village. Santell released the stone from his hand while the tension drained from him. He felt Melissa relax and turning to her, saw that her face was close, only inches from his own.

For a moment their eyes locked and then he murmured, "A close one," and got to his feet.

She followed and they returned to the horses.

"Funny thing," he said thoughtfully, after they once again were underway and the danger from Cunningham was gone, "how not having a gun can keep a man from getting into worse trouble. Back there in the village, a gun would have set things off for sure. Just now with that deputy, I probably would have shot him out of the saddle when he started for us. But having no gun, I didn't. He turned off and caused us no worry."

"A gun never settles anything, it only starts more of it. My father used to say that," Melissa said softly.

He gave her a straight-on look. "Why, yes, I guess that's about right," he said. "You kill a man, he's always got friends or relatives looking to even things up."

He turned away then, throwing a glance at the dark row of trees into which Sam Cunningham had ridden. "We better be careful for a spell," he said. "Cunningham might take a notion to come back."

She said, "All right, Clay," but she did not change her gaze toward him. Her deep eyes were upon him and she was having her thoughts about this man Santell who rode at her side. He was a savage, violent man, she suspected, but one of hidden, strange convictions and qualities. One who would turn and risk his life to aid a chance acquaintance who had done him a good turn. He was running now, actually running for his life, but she knew that was not of his own choosing but because of her. Had she not been on his hands, dependent upon him, he would have turned on his pursuers and made his stand.

It reminded her of a story her father had once told of a lone, fierce wolf, the last of his pack, who had come face to face at last with a dozen big, bloodthirsty hounds. Outnumbered, the old wolf had turned for the hills with the dogs after him. When they would draw too close, he would pause and fight them off, drive them back. Then he would run again for the safety of the hills. Time after time he made his stand, taking his toll of the dogs, but finally they downed him. There were just too many. He was outnumbered.

And that was the way it would be with Santell. Were she not along he likely, far back, probably at the old way station, would have come to bay and made his stand. He would have fought it out with Harry Decket and Jake Perrick and the others. He would have exacted his price but in the end he would have gone down into the dust with them. Outnumbered. He would be dead.

She shuddered at the thought. And suddenly she was glad she was with him; glad that she was hindering him and keeping him from halting and fighting a hopeless battle with Decket and his posse. This way, at least he was alive. She was keeping him so.

She wondered how he truly felt about it. Was he resenting the inconvenience of having her with him? Blaming her because her presence prevented him from halting and making a fight of it? She wondered and after a time she knew it didn't really matter. The important thing was that he was alive and so long as they kept running, striving to reach Splendor where his friend was and where there were other people to turn to for help, she didn't care. He would be alive; maybe he would never forgive her, for men have an odd way of looking at matters that pertain to their honor and reflect on their courage. But she could bear that; he would still be alive.

They maintained their pace, an easy gallop now. Santell wanted to favor the horses all they could and it was best they make as good a time as possible in the early morning coolness. The ponies, although benefited by the rest and feed at Lucero's, were still not in good condition but they were at least on a par with those of Decket and the posse, which had received only fragmentary breaks in their traveling. In a headlong chase, which this could well turn out to be at this stage, he felt certain their horses could keep up. But it was something you could not count on wholly. The outlaws had used their horses badly and a crippled horse went down fast when pushed too hard.

About them and on the prairie surrounding the wash, there were few signs left of the rain. The previous day's fierce wind had sucked away most all traces except for an occasional shallow puddle in the bed of the arroyo where they rode. There was a brighter greenness along the roots of the purple-tasseled grass which sparked with dew and the mesquite and dove weed looked somewhat fresher. Larks were awakening, whistling loudly from the tufts and flinging themselves wildly away when the horses came too close.

"Be another day without water and grub," Santell said, cocking his head at Melissa. He was almost cheerful about it, the proximity of Splendor lightening his mood. "Last one ever, I hope."

"Will we reach there by dark, you think?"

"If nobody tries heading us off."

The horses had begun to breathe heavily from the steady run. Santell drew them down to a walk and slid off his pony's back. Melissa immediately followed his example, hurrying forward to be at his side. Riding bareback was far from comfortable and walking could be a welcome change. They moved along and were still on foot when the sun broke over the low, eastern horizon and sent its warming rays flooding, like long fingers of color, across the land.

Santell eyed the heavens speculatively. "Going to be a hot one. That's all we need. We've had rain and wind and sand. All it takes is a scorcher to give us a taste of everything in the book."

He stopped suddenly, throwing out his arm to check Melissa. The horses crowded up against them and halted.

Just a few yards away a man and a horse lay prone on the arroyo's rocky bed.

17

In the early quiet Melissa whispered, "Who is it? One of Decket's men?"

Santell shook his head. He was thinking, this could be some sort of trick; a ruse of the marshal's to stop us so he could close in and nab us. But in the next moment he brushed that thought from his mind. The horse was dead. It looked like an accident for certain. And the man was none of the posse. He said, "Stranger to me."

He ground-reined the ponies and walked slowly toward the prostrate shapes, Melissa at his elbow. His keen glance covered the man thoughtfully, noting the good but well worn clothing, observing that no gunbelt encircled his waist, that he still clutched tightly a rifle in his right hand. He glanced briefly at the horse; it had been a fine animal — a bay gelding with strong, powerful legs and a deep chest.

They had come off the edge of the arroyo in a hurry, Santell surmised. The bay had been running fast in unfamiliar country, since they were unaware apparently of the wash that lay beyond that innocent-looking band of brush. The fall had broken the bay's neck and it looked as if it had about done for the rider as well.

The man groaned and moved slightly. Melissa said, "He's still alive!" and dropped to her knees near him.

Santell moved to the rider's opposite side and bending down, turned him over onto his back. A gasp slipped from Melissa's lips.

"Not a pretty sight," Santell commented dryly.

The man's jaws were heavily stubbled with coarse black whiskers. His mouth was a thick-lipped sneer and a wide scar stitched from temple to chin on one side of his square face. He had struck his head against the rocks of the arroyo in the fall and blood still trickled from a cut in his forehead.

Melissa said nothing. She rose and taking her handkerchief, stepped to one of the numerous shallow pools of rainwater. Soaking the bit of cloth she returned and after folding it into a compress, laid it on the injured man's head.

He stirred and opened his eyes, flat, colorless pockets that had neither content nor depth. He tried to rise, stubborn in his efforts, but still no expression on his face betrayed his true feelings — neither joy at being alive nor fear of being found. Only a pushing desire and determination, it appeared, to be up and on his way.

Melissa pressed him back firmly, wiping at his forehead with the damp cloth. He settled down, staring at her with a fixed resignation, seemingly trying to understand where he was and what had happened. He was still partly dazed. His stare drifted to Santell hunched at his opposite shoulder.

Santell said, "You had a bad spill, friend. Better lay there a bit longer."

There was suspicion in the rider's voice. "Who are you?"

"Name of Santell. Might ask the same of you."

The man continued to search Santell's features, saying finally, "Merrit. Jim Merrit."

"The lady is Miss Melissa York," Santell finished out the introductions. "Where you headed?"

Again there was a pause while the man who called himself Merritt considered the question. "Texas. Got me a good job waitin' there if I can make it."

"You must have been moving mighty fast on that horse. Any special reason?"

Merritt moved and shrugged. "Nope, no special reason. You know how it is with a good horse in the mornin'. Always like to run and act a fool."

"Reckon that bay's running days are over."

Merritt's empty stare came back quickly to Santell. "Meanin'?"

"Meaning he's dead. Broke his neck when he hit the rocks. Didn't you see this arroyo?"

"Would I be layin' here now with a dead horse if I had?" Merritt demanded angrily. "All I remember was ridin' along at a good clip and next thing I was pitchin' through the air. Then I wake up and see you folks."

Merritt grinned at Melissa, a hard-cornered, forced grimace. "Reckon I can set up now, ma'am."

Melissa moved back and the rider came to a sitting position. He was a big, wide-shouldered man, built much along the same lines as Santell. Except for the wide scar running down his cheek and the ugliness of his eyes, he was not a bad-looking man.

He reached first for the rifle, still lying at his side. Picking it up he checked it over carefully, levering the action and examining the end of the barrel to assure himself no damage had been done. "Sure could have messed up this gun," he said, laying it across his lap. Then, "You folks headed east for Texas, too?"

"Yes," Melissa replied.

"You got horses?" he asked quickly, too quickly Santell thought.

"A pair of pretty poor ones," she said. "Our own horses were stolen a couple nights ago. The thieves left two old nags in their place."

Merritt chuckled. "First time I ever heard of horse thieves leavin' horses," he observed. Taking the rifle up again, he got slowly to his feet. He was somewhat unsteady at first but after a minute he was all right.

He turned to Santell. "Hope you don't mind waitin' a bit. Like to travel along with you folks, if you don't mind. We're all goin' to Texas, seems."

Santell's voice was a little curt. "We don't have much time to lose. And we don't have a horse that can carry double. Fact is, neither one of them can hardly carry single."

At once Melissa broke in. "We can't just leave him here, Clay! He's still hurt. He can ride my horse and I'll walk."

The impatience was plain on Santell's dark face. "Not much time left for anybody to be walking," he said and turning on his heel, strode away.

Merritt gave Melissa his hard grin. "I'm obliged to you, ma'am. Don't want to cause no trouble 'twixt you and your friend, though. Maybe you'd better just go along and forget all about me. I'll make out somehow."

Melissa shook her head vigorously. "Nobody leaves an injured man alone on the prairies. It just isn't human."

"Well, I sure do appreciate it," Merritt drawled. "I'll try not to be no trouble."

He swung his glance to where Santell stood at the edge of the arroyo, his gaze fixed upon the trees far to the south and west. "You all in a big hurry to reach Texas?"

"Yes," Melissa said.

"That have somethin' to do with that shootin' I heard back there in the village early this mornin'?" Merritt's glance was sly as he swung back from Santell and settled upon the horses. They were grazing now on the grass that grew along the arroyo's bank. He was looking them over carefully, sizing them up, estimating their values. The rifle hung loosely in the crook of his arm.

Melissa turned her attention briefly to Santell and then back to Merritt. "Yes, it was. We're in trouble! Terrible trouble. There's a marshal back there looking for Clay — for Santell. He claims Clay is his escaped prisoner and he and a posse have been following us day and night, trying to catch up. They'll kill him if they do! That's why we're in such a hurry."

"That marshal — man by the name of Harry Decket?"

Melissa looked up in surprise. "You know him?"

Merritt said, hastily, "Heard of him. Heard he was in the country." He paused. "What's your deal here? I take it you're not married up with this Santell. How come you with him?"

"Some trouble of my own. Clay helped me. I was on my way back home, to Missouri."

"I see," Merritt said with a faint grin. "Looks like your friend Santell is in a tight spot. This Decket, I hear, is a mighty mean *hombre.*"

"You could help us," Melissa said impulsively, earnestly. "You've got a gun. We don't have anything to fight with. You could help us get to Texas."

"How's that, ma'am?"

"If Decket and his posse start getting too close, you could do some shooting and make them halt. Make them keep their distance until we reached help."

"Help? Who?"

"The marshal in Splendor. He's a friend of Clay's. If we can get to him before Decket stops us, Clay can prove he's not Shotgun Travers, the escaped prisoner Decket claims he is. They'll leave us alone then."

"Pretty slick, this Decket. Loses his real prisoner and so he tries to stick another man in his place!"

"He's a cruel and terrible man!" Melissa said with a shudder.

"Kind of runs in lawmen," Merritt said, his voice harsh. "They're all just like that. Think they're little kings."

His gaze was still on the horses. Melissa, noting this, said, "They aren't much, are they? But maybe they'll get us to Splendor."

"Don't bank on it. Appears to me best thing your friend can do is stand and fight it out."

208

"Stand and fight it out?" Melissa echoed in a horrified voice. "Against five men with no gun of any kind?"

"I got a gun," Merritt said, moving the rifle suggestively.

"But just one gun —"

"One's all we need. It would be easy. Set us a neat little trap and drop the marshal. Then you'd see how quick a posse can fall apart."

Santell had turned away from his post at the edge of the arroyo and was returning. He halted beside Melissa. To Merritt he said, "You feel like moving on?"

"Just as you say," the man replied, looking at Melissa.

"You don't want to walk, you can ride one of the horses for a spell. Got to save them all we can, however. The main thing is we can't stay here any longer."

Melissa suddenly confronted him. "Clay, he thinks we ought to stop and have a showdown with Decket and his posse."

Santell's brows lifted. "That so?"

"Sure," Merritt broke in. "I figure we would just wait for them to come up and then spring us a little surprise. We'll make them stand and listen. Explain who you are and all that."

"They wouldn't listen before," Santell said

curtly. "What makes you think they'll listen now?"

"This," Merritt said and patted the rifle. "If it comes to a fight, we got a good chance here in this wash. Out there on the flats they'd have us cold."

"Us?" Santell echoed.

Merritt nodded. "I got no cause to like this Decket. Or any lawman. I'll side you."

"You know Decket?" Santell asked, eyeing the big man closely.

"Heard of him," Merritt replied in that cautious way.

"I told him your trouble, all about the marshal and what he was trying to do," Melissa explained. "He wants to help us, Clay."

"I've got my own reasons for not wanting a showdown," Santell said stiffly.

"I know that. I know it is because of me. But it's different now. You've got somebody to help you, someone that can. And, like he said, if we got trapped out there on the prairie — oh, Clay! I don't want anything to happen to you!"

"It won't," Santell murmured, his manner changing perceptibly.

He swung back to Merritt. "Maybe you've got the right idea and I'm obliged to you for the offer. Be a little hard, however, for one man to hold off five armed men."

Merritt spat. "Not hard. Maybe risky, but not hard. I been there before. Like I said, we'll invite them to talk and listen. Then if Decket is hard-nosed about it, we'll show him we mean business."

"How?"

"Shoot him — what else?"

"Just kill him — in cold blood?" Melissa asked in a shocked voice.

"Reckon that's just what he's plannin' for your friend Santell, ma'am."

Santell shook his head slowly. "I don't want any man's blood on my hands, Merritt. In a fair draw and fight, it's all right. But this is another thing."

"I'll be holdin' the rifle, not you," Merritt said.

Santell considered for a minute, his face working while he studied upon the problem. "No," he said finally, "I still think the best answer is to try and reach Splendor. That way we maybe can avoid a killing. And another thing you want to remember, Merritt; we're not alone in this. We've got to think of Melissa."

"Maybe," Merritt said in an oily, suggestive way, "you just don't cotton to standin' up against Decket. Or any man."

Santell's gray eyes swept the man speculatively. "Maybe," he murmured softly. "But I've been thinking about something else. Like you could be looking for a chance to even up something with Harry Decket and you're trying to make use of us in doing it. Seems to me you know a lot about the marshal you're not mentioning."

"Maybe," Merritt replied cagily. "Just could be you're right."

Melissa's voice suddenly cut through the descending tense hush that followed Merritt's words.

"Clay! The posse! They're coming!"

18

Santell quickly turned his attention to the flat lands beyond the arroyo. Five riders coming abreast, not a mile distant. They must have ridden within the strip of trees to get so close without being noticed. That they were still unaware of Santell and the others was evident.

"What'll it be, cowboy? Fight or run? Better make up your mind."

Santell came back to Merritt. A suspicion had been growing in his mind, one augmented by the scraps of information and small hints the big man had dropped during their conversation.

"Little late to run," he said slowly, "something you likely figured on while you kept us here talking."

"Could be just so," Merritt said easily.

"And maybe your name's not Merritt at all but Shotgun Travers!"

The scar-faced man laughed. "You sure catch on fast!" He fell back a step, lifting the rifle.

A small cry came from Melissa. She moved to Santell's side, seizing his arm. Her eyes were wide with horror and distress. "Oh, Clay! I'm sorry! It was my fault for telling him — for getting you into this!"

Santell laid his hand comfortingly upon hers. "It's all right, Melissa. Don't worry. It'll work out."

"No fault of yours, ma'am," Travers said then. "Reckon the cards just had to fall this way. Been hopin' for a chance to square up with Harry Decket. Promised him I'd do just that some day. Guess this happens to be it."

He lifted his flat, expressionless glance to the rim of the arroyo, to the approaching posse now much closer. "Never expected to have no cinch deal like this, though."

Santell said, "You've got no reason to keep the girl here. Let her take one of the horses and leave while there's still time."

Melissa immediately shook her head. "I'm staying with you, Clay. No matter what you say — I'm staying. I won't leave!"

"You're sure right, ma'am," Travers said agreeably. "You're stayin'. Why I've got it figured your friend Santell is my ticket to Decket there. And you're my insurance that Santell will stay and do what I tell him."

Santell's face hardened into bleak planes. "You've got no reason to hurt her, Travers!"

"No? Well, you do just what I tell you and she don't get hurt. Leastwise, not by me."

He lifted his gaze again to the prairie. "Reckon we better get our little reception committee ready," he said. Abruptly the man's affability dropped away and his voice switched to a hard-edged command. "Now, you two walk right over there against that bank, facing Decket and his friends. When they get in sight you raise your hands and holler. You're wantin' to surrender. Understand?"

Santell nodded. "And?"

"I'll be right across this ditch from you. I'll have this rifle on the girl all the time. One funny move out of you to cross me up and she gets a bullet in her pretty hide."

Under the waving muzzle of the rifle Santell and Melissa took up their assigned positions against the arroyo's wall. Watching them narrowly, Travers crossed to a point directly opposite and crouched down beneath the overhanging bank of the wash. His plan was simple; he would remain hidden until Decket and the others, drawn by Melissa and Santell, halted on the bank a few feet over his head. At the proper moment he would leap out, gun blazing. The close range coupled with the element of surprise would make him a deadly executioner.

Travers settled down, not sitting on his haunches but waiting on half-bent knees, thereby being in a stance that would permit his moving faster. He grinned across the fifteen-foot interval to Santell and Melissa.

"Right cozy, ain't it?"

"It is murder!" Melissa said with tremor. "Cold-blooded murder!"

"Better them than me," Travers replied. "Ain't much to killin' a man. Maybe the first time. After that it don't amount to nothin'. Anyway, man's got a right to protect himself."

Over the rim of the arroyo Santell could see the steady approach of the posse. They were close enough to make them out now. Decket and Perrick were at one end of the line, the near end. Next came Charley Ironhead, then Cunningham, and last of all, Tex

London. They were riding leisurely, spread out not far apart, looking more like ranchers on their way to a cattlemen's meeting than five grim lawmen on a manhunt.

"Clay," Melissa said softly at his side, "I'm sorry about all this, about everything. Seems like I've been nothing but trouble for you since the night we met. It's my fault you're in a terrible fix like this."

He took her hand. "You didn't get me into this. Decket was my problem. You had nothing to do with that."

"But if it hadn't been for me you might have gotten away that first night, been free of all this now. I don't think either of us will come out of this alive. If Decket and Jake Perrick don't kill us, he will."

"Don't give up yet," Santell replied. "It may not all go the way Travers figures."

"But if it does, Clay, I want you to know this — that I love you."

He turned to face her, the wonder of her words stirring him deeply. Raising his arm he placed it about her shoulders and drew her close. "I never thought — I never hoped —" he began and halted uncertainly, entangled in his own emotions.

She came to his rescue, giving him her sweet smile. "I know. I understand what you're trying to say. We've both been such fools! Holding back when we should have been living the time that was ours but we could not or would not see. I was afraid and you — you were always so far away, thinking of someone else, another girl."

"Another girl!" he echoed bitterly. "Yes, I was doing that, I admit. Of a girl who led me on for a long time and then turned a knife in me by marrying my best friend! I swore then I never again would listen to a woman's words and let her get under my hide. I wanted nothing to do with any woman. When we met, I took it to be one of those accidents, something I couldn't avoid. And so I tried to make the best of it."

"And all the time I thought there was another girl, one you were remembering and going back to."

He shook his head. "This comes a little late, Melissa, but I will say it. In only a day and a couple of nights you've come to mean more to me than anyone or anything in this world. If we get out of this, there's one thing I promise — I'll make up for all the lost time!"

He kissed her then, ignoring the leering, scarred face of Shotgun Travers watching them from across the narrow interval of arroyo.

"That's mighty touchin'," he said, his

voice sagging with sarcasm. "Supposin' now we get down to business. Take a squint at that posse, Santell. Where is it? How far away?"

Santell threw his glance beyond the rim of the wash again. The posse was not in sight. He had a moment when his heart surged with hope. But a moment later he realized they had only dipped into a low swale, that they were still coming and had not swung to another direction.

"How far?" Travers pressed.

"Two hundred yards, more or less."

"How far?" Travers repeated; frankly disbelieving.

"Look for yourself," Santell shrugged.

"You try lyin' to me and your little gal friend gets hurt!" the outlaw warned.

"Then maybe you getter get up and see for yourself. I said about two hundred yards. That's where they are."

Travers settled back down, satisfied. Santell was casting about desperately in his mind for some plan to thwart the gunman. He had no love for Harry Decket and his men and had no cause to aid them, but he could not find it in his heart to stand by and watch the cold-blooded murder of five men — much less be a party to it. His life, he knew, was in danger either way and he doubted if Melissa was in any better position. Travers would leave no witnesses if he came out of the ambush with a whole skin. And Decket had given the order for his men to shoot Travers — or Santell, on sight. He might never live to give a warning, even if he wanted to.

"Maybe you two better be gettin' your hands in the air. High, so little ol' Harry can see them."

The posse was in full view now. Santell could see Charley Ironhead's sharp hawk-like face turned toward them. He had caught his first glimpse of them in the arroyo. Santell lifted his arms, holding them palms outward. Melissa did likewise. A plan had sprung into Santell's mind — a wild, desperate chance but at least it might tip off the posse and afford them enough time to save themselves and prevent Travers from escaping and ever again committing another murder.

He tipped his dark face down to Melissa. In a low voice he said, "Be ready. When I shove you, throw yourself behind that bush. There on your left."

"What are you going to do?" Melissa asked, her voice fearful.

"What's that?" Travers demanded sharply. "Don't try anything cute on me, Santell."

"Just telling the lady goodbye."

The posse had halted some seventy-five yards away. They were grouped in a tight little circle. Jake Perrick was talking while the others stared into the arroyo.

"Where's the marshal by now, Santell?"

Travers kept his voice low, indicating he suspected the riders were close.

"Hundred yards, maybe."

"Clay —" Melissa began and then stopped, her voice breaking.

"We won't say goodbye," he murmured. "This isn't the finish for us, Melissa. I've got a hunch we're coming out of this all right."

He wished he was as certain as his words sounded. But he would try to make it come true. That was all he could do. Nothing left to do but try.

The posse was advancing slowly, walking their horses, suspecting some trick. Apparently it was all too easy, too simple. It wasn't natural and understandable for Santell to elude them for two nights and a day and then suddenly, on the very verge of escape, surrender without a struggle. But Santell and Melissa were there in plain sight with their hands uplifted in a token of submission. What sort of a trap could it be?

"Santell — where are they?" Travers called softly.

"Thirty yards."

The dragging seconds ground interminably by. The sun was now up, its heat already beginning to make itself felt. Somewhere off to the left an insect clacked loudly in a doveweed bush. The noise of the horses cropping the thin grass along the arroyo's edge was a steady sound in the suspended hush.

Twenty yards . . .

Harry Decket's face was a grim, frozen mask, utterly devoid of expression. Perrick had a half-smile on his thick lips, his rifle ready in the crook of his arms. Santell wondered if the man was thinking of Melissa. Sam Cunningham rode still and sharply alert beside Tex London, who had a white cloth wrapped around his head. He seemed disinterested in the whole proceedings. Charley Ironhead, his birdlike, swarthy face and glittering black eyes definite in the strong sunlight, held slightly back, his suspicion bright and pronounced.

Ten yards . . .

"Travers!"

Perrick's voice reached out over the interval of flats into the arroyo. "Don't you be tryin' no tricks, Travers!"

Five yards . . .

Santell's glance dropped to the outlaw. He was crouched under the overhang. An evil grin cracked his face, drawing his lips back over his teeth. The sun shining on his dark features emphasized the smooth track of scar slashing through the stubble of whiskers. Travers watched him. He was taking no chances on Santell's crossing him up. Santell returned the stare of those terrible, empty eyes. The thought moved through him: *a man dies one time; better it be of his own choosing than letting it fritter away in a bed.*

"Travers!" Harry Decket's voice was a high-pitched snarl.

"Now!" Santell hissed to Melissa and thrust her, hard, into the brush. In the next breath he yelled, "Look out! Ambush!"

He leaped forward, bending and ducking sideways. He scooped up loose sand with both hands. Continuing the upsweeping motion, he threw it straight into Shotgun Travers' face. In that same fleeting fragment of time, almost in unison, Travers and Perrick fired. A solid force smashed into Santell's shoulder. He went over and slammed down hard onto his back. Which bullet had struck him he did not know.

He watched Travers spin out from beneath

the overhang. He dropped to one knee, firing as he moved. Harry Decket went out of his saddle as if struck by a giant's hand. Guns were cracking in a wild confusion of sound and smoke. Santell saw puffs of dust lift from Travers' coat. The outlaw continued to shoot but his bullets were going wide, almost straight up. He tipped slowly backward. Suddenly the rifle became too heavy for him. He let it sink to the sand beside him.

Perrick and Cunningham, guns ready, came down from their horses and dropped cautiously into the wash.

"What kind of a stunt was that, Travers?" Perrick demanded, walking to where Santell lay. Melissa had crawled from the brush, bruised and scratched but otherwise unharmed. She had taken Santell's head into her lap and was stroking his stubbled cheek slowly.

"Travers?" the outlaw laughed thickly from his place on the sand. "Hell, you fat-gut, he's not Travers. That's me."

Perrick wheeled about. "What's that?"

"I'm Travers. I'm the boy your tin-horn marshal was lookin' for. That man over there was just his substitute."

"Then how — why —"

"You just study about it for a spell,"

Travers said, his words coming more slowly and with greater effort. His voice had a bubbling sound. "Some of these days maybe you'll get it all figured out. You want to know who I am. I'm Shotgun Travers . . . Look my picture up in the first sheriff's office you come to."

From the top of the bank Tex London's voice, sounding oddly muffled as if he were speaking through clenched teeth, said, "Decket's dead."

"That's good . . . mighty good," Travers muttered and slumped back.

"Then we was chasin' the wrong man all the time!" Perrick exclaimed. "And that danged little marshal knew it."

"Looks like he sure played us for suckers," Sam Cunningham said. He walked to where Melissa and Santell were. "Can I help you any with him, ma'am?"

"If you'll catch up our horses," she replied, "I think we can manage after that."

The wound was not bad. By the time Cunningham was back, Melissa had it bound up and Santell was on his feet, unsteady but able to walk.

"Bring that there horse of the marshal's down here, Tex," Perrick called over his shoulder. "We got to load this body on. Horse will have to carry them both, I reckon, but the marshal don't weigh much."

He turned then to Melissa and Santell. Santell had picked up Travers' rifle and was holding it crossed over his left forearm. Perrick glanced at the gun.

"Hope we ain't goin' to have no trouble, Santell," he said, his face turning stiff. "I'm real sorry we caused you what we did. You too, Miss York . . . Is there anything I can be doin' for you?"

Santell felt Melissa's fingers tighten upon his wrist and turning, saw the pleading in her eyes. He shrugged and without answering the man, turned to his horse.

"No hard feelin's?" Perrick persisted.

Santell paused in the effort to climb onto his mount. "No hard feelings — long as you stay in your town. There's a few things I'm not soon forgetting. Best for you we don't meet again."

"Sure, sure," Perrick said, the tension going out of his bulky shape, leaving him slack again. "I reckon you two are figurin' on marryin' up."

Santell glanced at Melissa. She was smiling at him from her place on her horse. He thought it was the most beautiful sight he had ever seen. He nodded. "So?"

"Splendor — I was just thinkin' that was

a fine name for a marryin' town," Perrick said.

Santell grinned. That was one thing he could agree with Jake Perrick on.

ABOUT THE AUTHOR

Ray Hogan was born in Missouri but has spent most of his life in New Mexico. His father was an early Western marshal and lawman, and Hogan himself has spent a lifetime researching the West. He has written over 100 books, including OUTLAW'S PLEDGE, PILGRIM, THE HELL RAISER, THE DOOMSDAY TRAIL, DECISION AT DOUBTFUL CANYON, and 24 titles in the bestselling Shawn Starbuck series, all available in Signet paperback. His work has been filmed, televised, and translated into sixteen languages.

We hope you have enjoyed this Large Print book. Other Thorndike, Wheeler, Kennebec, and Chivers Press Large Print books are available at your library or directly from the publishers.

For information about current and upcoming titles, please call or write, without obligation, to:

Publisher
Thorndike Press
295 Kennedy Memorial Drive
Waterville, ME 04901
Tel. (800) 223-1244

or visit our Web site at:

http://gale.cengage.com/thorndike

OR

Chivers Large Print
published by BBC Audiobooks Ltd
St James House, The Square
Lower Bristol Road
Bath BA2 3SB
England
Tel. +44(0) 800 136919
email: bbcaudiobooks@bbc.co.uk
www.bbcaudiobooks.co.uk

All our Large Print titles are designed for easy reading, and all our books are made to last.